"What about you, Lacon? Don't you want things to be different for you?"

"What makes you think I want anything different from what I have right now?" he said.

Maybe he didn't. Maybe Marissa had misjudged him. "I don't know. You just seem a little lonely when it's quiet like this and no one needs rescuing."

Lacon reached out, tugged at a wisp of her curly hair. "How could I be lonely with you standing right there?"

His fingertips traced Marissa's cheek, trailed down her throat, moved around her neck and pulled her close. Her breath caught but she didn't resist. Deep down she'd wanted to know what he tasted like from the moment they met. His lips closed over hers and the taste of wine and man had her melting against him.

Lacon drew away all too soon. "We're not crossing that line tonight, Issy."

She curled her fingers in his shirtfront and held him close when he would have moved away. Her voice was thick with the desire sizzling in her veins. "We're both adults. We can do whatever we like..."

BODY OF EVIDENCE

USA TODAY Bestselling Author

DEBRA WEBB

This book is dedicated to the amazing nurses and doctors we often take for granted. Thank you so much for all you do.

ISBN-13: 978-1-335-52646-5

Body of Evidence

PLEASE RECYCLE • THIS PRODUCT IS RECYCLABLE •

Recycling programs for this product may not exist in your area.

This edition published by arrangement with Harlequin Books S.A.

For questions and comments about the quality of this book, please contact us at CustomerService@Harlequin.com.

Printed in U.S.A.

Debra Webb is the award-winning *USA TODAY* bestselling author of more than one hundred novels, including those in reader-favorite series Faces of Evil, the Colby Agency and the Shades of Death. With more than four million books sold in numerous languages and countries, Debra's love of storytelling goes back to childhood on a farm in Alabama. Visit Debra at www.debrawebb.com.

Books by Debra Webb

Harlequin Intrigue

Colby Agency: Sexi-ER

Finding the Edge
Sin and Bone
Body of Evidence

Faces of Evil

Dark Whispers
Still Waters

Colby Agency: The Specialists

Bridal Armor
Ready, Aim...I Do!

Colby, TX

Colby Law
High Noon
Colby Roundup

Debra Webb writing with Regan Black

Harlequin Intrigue

Colby Agency: Family Secrets

Gunning for the Groom

The Specialists: Heroes Next Door

The Hunk Next Door
Heart of a Hero
To Honor and To Protect
Her Undercover Defender

Visit the Author Profile page at Harlequin.com.

CAST OF CHARACTERS

Dr. Marissa Frasier—An outstanding ER doctor at the state-of-the-art facility called the Edge. When Marissa wakes up with her ex-husband dead in the bed beside her, she needs the kind of help only the Colby Agency can provide.

Lacon Traynor—Lacon is one of the Colby Agency's best. He will do whatever it takes to protect Marissa Frasier, even if it means losing his heart in the process.

Vito Anastasia—One of the most notorious gangsters in Chicago. If Vito has his way, Marissa will become his no matter how many people have to die to make it happen.

Dr. William Bauer—How far will he go to have revenge against his ex-wife, Marissa Frasier?

Victoria Colby-Camp—The head of the prestigious Colby Agency.

Detectives Nader and Watts—Chicago PD is working overtime to connect all the murders, including Marissa Frasier's dead ex-husband, to the murderer—unfortunately, Marissa is their top suspect.

Chapter One

The Edge Emergency Department, Chicago
Thursday, June 28, 9:30 p.m.

Dr. Marissa Frasier ruffled the hair of her six-year-old patient, Jeremiah Owens. "You were very brave, Jeremiah."

The little boy had arrived at the ER two hours ago with a greenstick fracture to the radius about three inches above his left wrist. After an examination and then X-rays to confirm, he had stoically watched as Dr. Pete Myers, the ortho on call, applied the cast for keeping the arm stable. Jeremiah had chosen royal blue for his cast. Though there had been no serious shift in the bones as a result of the fracture, they wanted it to stay that way, and children couldn't always be counted on to follow instructions or to keep on a splint. A cast was typically the better route to go with younger patients.

The child's lips had quivered and his eyes had

grown bright during the procedure, but Mom was the only one who cried. The poor woman had apologized profusely. Her sweet son had repeatedly told her that he was okay and that it didn't really hurt. Being a parent was difficult at times, and this had been one of those times.

Dr. Myers had quickly moved on to an elderly patient who'd arrived with a fracture to the upper quarter of the femur. Never a good thing, but particularly problematic in older patients. Apparently tonight's theme was broken bones. They'd had three others this evening. Marissa was reasonably confident that was a record for a Thursday night.

"Thank you, Doctor," Mrs. Owens said, her tears all but dry now. "He was a very brave boy." She kissed the top of her child's head.

Marissa smiled. "Perhaps when Nurse Bowman has gone over the dismissal instructions, a reward is in order for your outstanding bravery, Jeremiah."

"I think that's a very good idea." His mother patted him gently on the back. "A reward would be very nice, don't you think, Jeremiah?"

He nodded eagerly, the hint of a smile tugging at the corners of his mouth.

"Nurse Bowman will let you pick something from our special treasure chest." Marissa gave Eva a nod as she walked to the door. "Have a safe drive home."

This time Jeremiah actually flashed her a real

smile. She couldn't decide whether he was happier about the treasure chest or going home.

The ER had been buzzing for the past several hours. A couple had misjudged the time it would take to reach their preferred hospital and ended up having to stop at the Edge for their little girl's entrance into the world. A two-car accident with five victims; a bicycle crash involving two teenagers who suffered broken bones, nasty lacerations and no shortage of bruises; and two concertgoers who'd taken tumbles while crowd surfing had shown up with fractures similar to Jeremiah's. There was also a knife fight between two thugs in a drug deal gone wrong. Both victims had arrived in the backs of police cruisers.

And yet another little boy, Timmy, who arrived with a scary-looking laceration to the upper arm, caused by a bad idea. The boy had decided he wanted to practice knife throwing the way a character in some movie he'd watched recently had done. Amazingly he had actually hit the tree with the knife he'd sneaked from his mother's kitchen. The trouble had occurred when he braced his left arm against the tree and attempted to dislodge the knife with his right, slicing across his left arm only a couple of inches above the elbow. He was a very lucky little boy. A little deeper, and he might not have arrived at the ER in time. The brachial artery was closest to the surface near the elbow. Marissa was very thankful the injury was not so deep and had missed the artery.

At the double doors that led back into the lobby, Jeremiah slipped free from his mother's hand and raced back to where Marissa stood near the nurses' station and gave her a hug. She crouched down and hugged him back. Her heart reacted. She had so wanted children of her own.

Not meant to be. At least not so far, and with no prospects of a boyfriend, much less a husband, the outlook was rather dim.

When the child skipped back to where his mother waited at the open door, Marissa waved goodbye. As the doors closed, she turned back to the chart she was reviewing.

"Dr. Frasier."

Marissa paused and looked up at the registration specialist, Patsy Tanner, who'd called her name. "Yes, Patsy?"

"There's a man in the lobby who says he needs to see you." She shrugged. "I told him you were with a patient but he just keeps pacing the room. He asks for you every five or so minutes." Her expression turned uncertain. "He looks very upset."

A frown furrowing its way across her weary forehead, Marissa dredged up a smile. "Thank you, Patsy. I'll take care of it."

Sometimes a father or husband or even boyfriend of a patient would grow agitated and demand to speak with the doctor who had cared for his loved one. Since Marissa hadn't lost any patients or even attended to any patients with a dire prognosis this evening, she couldn't imagine the trouble would be too serious. Perhaps one of the two who'd been carried off to jail after their knife battle had a disgruntled friend. She sent a quick text to Security and asked that they keep an eye on the situation as she spoke with the man pacing the lobby.

The moment Marissa stepped beyond the double doors that stood between those waiting for care and the emergency department, she knew it wasn't going to be so easy.

Even before the man turned around, she recognized him. The rigid set of his broad shoulders. The silky dark brown hair that brushed his collar. He wore jeans and a shirt, not the khakis and a polo he'd preferred before their lives had fallen apart. William Bauer turned around as if he sensed her presence, despite the fact that eight or nine other people were scattered around the room, speaking softly or searching their social media feeds on their phones.

It had been that way between them in the beginning. Even a few hours apart had felt like an eternity. They had sensed each other across a crowded room, their hearts seeming to beat harder and harder until they touched.

Marissa's ex-husband strode toward her, his gaze narrowing, homing in on her. The anger twisting his lips—the lips she had kissed so many times—warned this would not be a pleasant visit by any definition of the word. Unfortunately, this was not his first unannounced appearance, and she feared it would not be his last.

When he stalled toe-to-toe with her, his six-foot-two form looming over her five-foot-six one, she asked, “Why are you here, William?”

“You changed your cell number. I had no choice.”

Thankfully he kept his voice down, but there was no mistaking the fury in his tone.

Marissa glanced around the room. “Why don’t we step outside where we’ll have some privacy?”

The subtle shift in his posture told her he liked the idea of privacy. Uneasiness pricked her, but security was nearby. Her ex-husband stepped back, allowing her to go ahead of him. She moved toward the exit, keeping her step steady and her smile pleasant. No need to let anyone see the worry and the dread pulsing beneath her skin.

She and William had been married for five years. The first year had felt happy, or at least as happy as any two people with newly minted medical degrees diving into their residencies could feel. More often than not they were either flying high with adrenaline or utterly drained from exhaustion. They had married at the courthouse the day after they finished medical school. Miracle of miracles, the NRMP, National Resident Matching Program, had matched them both to hospitals in the Chicago area. A whirlwind trip to the city had ended with them leasing the cheapest apartment they could find, and they'd been completely thrilled that it had a reasonably large shower, a bedroom and was near both their hospitals.

Then, slowly but surely, everything had changed.

Marissa had done exceedingly well. She'd garnered praise and numerous opportunities for her hard work. William, on the other hand, had floundered. He couldn't seem to keep up. His work was subpar. He didn't get along with anyone. He'd barely survived his residency. By the end of the second year, they had argued every minute they were together, which wasn't nearly enough to sustain a relationship.

A little less than two years ago, he had been asked to leave the practice he'd joined after residency. It was either he leave voluntarily, or legal steps would be taken to remove him. The senior doctor in the practice was a mutual friend. Though Marissa and William had already been divorced for a couple of months by then, he'd called to explain that he had grave concerns about William's mental health.

Sadly, he hadn't been telling Marissa anything new. The breakdown in their marriage had mirrored the disintegration of his mental health. Twenty-three months and two weeks ago, he'd finally snapped and he'd turned physical. Marissa had ended up with a concussion and a fractured arm much like little Jeremiah's. At her ex-husband's trial, the judge had been particularly peeved by the fact that William was a doctor, and subsequently sentenced him to a year for felony domestic violence. He'd been released six months ago.

The first thing he'd done was come to Marissa and apologize for his behavior. Since that time he'd been volunteering in the community and appeared to be working hard to redeem himself. Marissa had no idea how he was earning any sort of income. He'd exhausted the meager savings they had managed prior to the divorce with his need to prove his status with a new car every year. Unfortunately, his salary as a general practitioner was not that of a cardiothoracic surgeon, as he appeared to want the world to believe.

However much he wanted to act as if he had learned his lesson, Marissa knew better. He was still drinking. Before and, foolishly, even after the divorce, she had tried to help him, but she'd soon recognized that she could not help a man unwilling to help himself. No matter that they had been officially divorced for eighteen months and twenty-two days, he never left her alone for long.

In part, she blamed herself. If she'd made a clean break after he attacked her physically rather than attempting to help him, things might have been different. Now, no matter how many times she told him to back off, he always found a way to insert himself into her life. He discovered something among his things that belonged to her. A letter addressed to her had come to his apartment. A relative was ill and he thought she might want to know. When he'd run out of legitimate excuses, he'd started showing up simply to argue about how she had ruined his life.

She suspected this evening's visit was the latter, though he had never showed up at her ER before. Too many potential witnesses.

Once they were a few yards from the ER entrance but still within sight of the security guard who monitored that entrance, William lit into her.

"Why would you change your phone number? You've had the same number since we moved to Chicago."

He stood very close to her, his face so near she could feel his breath on her cheek, could smell the liquor when he spoke. William was a handsome man still. Classic square jaw, straight nose, nice lips, assessing brown eyes. But once things started to fall apart, his eyes were always bloodshot from the sheer volume of alcohol he consumed daily. The final year of their marriage, he would come home from work and drink until he passed out in his chair or on the sofa or wherever he happened to be when the saturation point of alcohol in his blood took control. It was as if he couldn't bear his life, so he attempted to wash away each day's memories with booze. Every month or so he would promise to join Alcoholics Anonymous. He even went *once.*

So ironic. He'd been the best all through high school. Best GPA. Best player on the football team. Best all-around student. Class president. College had been much the same. Even in medical school, he had been the golden boy among the professors and his peers. Never had to work very hard to achieve his class ranking.

Whether it all merely caught up with him in the end or he just couldn't keep up the pace any longer, he plummeted. From all reports, once he went into practice he was a satisfactory doctor. There had never been any complaints from patients. Certainly no malpractice suits. It was his colleagues who couldn't tolerate his bullying and bad behavior.

And his wife. For a while, Marissa had taken his mental abuse and, ultimately, his first and only departure into physical abuse. But that mistake would never be repeated. She refused to be a victim like that ever again. Granted, he had been drunk out of his mind at the time, but she would not allow him to use his drinking as an excuse. He had hurt her and that was that.

"I changed my number because I would like you to stop calling me." She kept her gaze steady on his. It was important that he understand her decision was not up for discussion. She knew this man intimately. At the moment he appeared reasonably sober, and she wanted him to see and to hear that she meant business. The life they had once shared was over. They were not friends, and they never would be.

"You've finally found someone else, haven't you?" Rage blazed in his dark eyes.

An alarm she knew better than to ignore triggered. There was something about his eyes, his tone that seemed different tonight—colder, harder. "This is not about anyone else, William. This is about you." She kept her voice steady, her tone firm. A year of counseling had helped her to overcome feelings of guilt about the breakdown of their marriage and to stand up for herself, even against the man she had once loved and with whom she had expected to spend the rest of her life. "Now, if you'll excuse me, I have to get back to my patients."

"Is that another kick in the teeth?" he growled. "I don't have a career anymore. No patients. No nothing."

She braced herself and summoned her waning courage. "You don't have a career anymore because you drink too much. You need help, William. I can't help you. Until you commit to changing your life, this is how it will be." She backed away a step. "You should go back to AA and seek private counseling."

He grabbed her arm, his fingers clutching like a vise. A wave of panic flooded her.

"Don't tell me what to do," he warned. "If you had been a better wife, maybe I wouldn't have needed to drink. You could have helped me, but you chose to throw me—our life—away."

It was the same exchange every time. When he grew angry, he always blamed someone else for his mistakes. "Goodbye, William." She yanked her arm from his grasp and turned away.

One day he would surely come to terms with the reality that *he* made his own choices, and *he* executed those choices.

"Issy."

She hesitated. Shouldn't have. Damn it.

"Look at me. Please."

How was it that she could still feel sympathy for this man? He had made her life miserable for four years before the divorce. He'd done his damnedest to do the same thing the past six months since his release from prison, but she had managed to handle it better. It was always easier to deal with issues from a distance. And though he insinuated himself into her present every chance he got, they did not share a home…they did not share a bed. He was no longer her responsibility, legally or morally.

She took a deep breath. Turned to face him. "First," she said, "if you ever touch me again, I will take out a restraining order, and then you'll have yet another black mark on your record. Now, what is it you want to say?"

He stared at her for a long moment. Even from several feet away, she could feel the sheer hatred emanating from him. The bright exterior lighting allowed her to see the desperation in his eyes. She shook her head and started to turn away but his lips parted and, once more, she hesitated.

"I'm going to kill myself."

Shock slammed into her gut. She sucked in a sharp breath. “You don’t mean that.”

He nodded. “I do.”

“Please, William, you need help. See someone before you destroy any chance of ever rebuilding your life and career. Everyone deserves a second chance. Give yourself one before it’s too late.”

He shook his head. “I’m going to kill myself. But first—” he stared at her so hard she could feel the cold, ruthless pressure of his fury “—I’m going to kill *you*.”

He walked away.

Marissa’s knees buckled, forcing her to grab for the sleek limestone wall to steady herself. She watched him settle behind the steering wheel of his car and drive away. As much as she wanted to believe that he was only attempting to frighten her, she knew better than to be that naive. As a physician, she was well aware that people could snap and do unspeakable things.

William had been teetering on the precipice of total self-destruction for years now. Her first obligation as a physician was to report the threat. Since he was no longer practicing medicine, that was one less concern. She would call the office of his former practice and let their mutual friend know about the threat he’d made. If William was so angry with her, it was highly probable that he felt a similar rage for his former colleagues.

Making her way back inside, she prepared a mental list of everyone she should call. Her brain raced with the idea that this wasn't supposed to happen to her. She had been a good student all through school. She'd never gotten involved with drugs or alcohol. Even in college and then medical school, she was the consummate Goody Two-shoes. Focused, reliable—that was Marissa Frasier. As her marriage fell apart, she'd endeavored patiently and persistently to try to repair their relationship. But nothing worked. When she had done all within her power, she had extracted herself from the ever-increasing volatility of the situation. He'd already destroyed her ability to love him. She'd felt sympathy—as she did now—but that was no basis for a marriage.

The waiting room was nearly clear now. Maybe things would slow down, giving her a chance to pull herself together once more. A few more deep breaths to slow her racing heart, and she was getting there. Once she was through the double doors and headed toward the nurses' station, she relaxed.

Eva caught her in the corridor before she reached the doctors' lounge. "Are you okay, Dr. Frasier?"

Marissa produced a smile. Eva was one of those people whom everyone liked. With her white-blond hair and creamy porcelain skin, many of the older patients called her an angel. But it was her green eyes that Marissa first noticed. Their eyes were a very similar emerald green. Marissa, too, had the extra-pale skin, but her fiery red curls set the two of them apart. Patients were always saying that if not for the difference in hair color, they could pass for sisters.

Marissa took her friend's hand and pulled her into the lounge. With a quick glance around she said, "It's William. He showed up again. *Here.*" She moistened her lips and wished her heart would not start that confounded pounding again. "It was different this time."

"Are you serious?" Eva took both Marissa's hands in hers. "Listen to me—this situation is not getting better. He's escalating. If you continue to interact with him—"

Marissa shook her head. "I won't. I can't." She inhaled a deep breath. "He said he's going to kill himself, but first he's going to kill me."

"That's it." Eva released her and reached into the pocket of her scrubs for her cell phone. "I'm calling Todd. You need protection."

Eva's fiancé was an investigator at the Colby Agency. Eva had urged her repeatedly to go to the agency for help about William. Somehow Marissa had been certain she could do this herself, but now she wasn't so sure.

His desperation and fury had been palpable. He was not playing.

He wanted her dead.

The bottom dropped out of Marissa's stomach and she wrapped her arms around her middle. How on earth had they gotten to this place? How could a man who had once loved her—and she knew in her heart that he had—now want to kill her?

She had no answer. William was broken. He had allowed envy and whatever other hidden mental health issues that plagued him to take over. Add the alcohol on top of that, and he was a mess. A desperate mess who didn't care anymore. He wanted the pain and misery to end, and he wanted the person he saw as responsible for that pain and misery to pay for ruining his life.

Eva was right. She couldn't handle this situation any longer. Now she was the one who needed help.

Eva ended her call. She took Marissa's hands once more and gave them a squeeze. "Victoria, the head of the agency I've been telling you about, will see you first thing in the morning—if that works for you."

Marissa nodded, her entire being numb. "I'll go. I can't ignore this situation any longer."

"You have to believe me when I say that Victoria will know what to do. Her agency helped me, and they helped Dr. Pierce. They can help you."

The first spring of tears burned her eyes, and Marissa cursed herself for being so weak. "Thank you."

"Listen," Eva said gently, "Todd and I don't want you to be alone tonight, so I'm taking you home with me."

"No." Marissa shook her head. "I can't do that. The two of you are just finding your way in your relationship. I don't want to intrude. I truly appreciate the offer, but really, I have a security system and I'd feel much better at home. I need to be able to think all this through and prepare for tomorrow's meeting."

"Okay, but if you need anything, all you have to do is call." Eva hugged her hard. Marissa closed her eyes and fought the damned tears.

This was not the time for her to fall apart. Staying alive and safe required her to keep it together. It was well past time she focused on taking care of herself.

Tomorrow she would take the necessary steps to purge William from her life once and for all.

Chapter Two

Hampden Court, Friday, June 29, 6:00 a.m.

The sound of traffic on the street outside her East Lincoln Park graystone woke Marissa. The room-darkening Roman shades she'd ordered when she first bought the house nearly two years ago did their job very well, ensuring that the room was pitch-black. Working nights more often than not at the ER required sleeping in the daytime. Not so easy to do without the darkness.

There were times when total darkness was a good thing.

This was her rare long weekend, so she could sleep in this morning. Her next scheduled shift was Tuesday. She intended to treat herself the next couple of days. Some long-overdue shopping, maybe a mani-pedi. She pulled the silky sheet close around her and toyed with the idea of actually sleeping in. How long had it been since she'd stayed in bed until noon unless she'd worked until seven or eight in the morning? Besides, the shops wouldn't open for hours.

Then she remembered William's cruel words—the angry promise that he was going to kill himself and her.

She had an appointment at the Colby Agency at nine. A weary sigh whispered across her lips. She should get up, shower and figure out something to wear. Well before her divorce, her social life had died a slow, suffocating death. It had been so long since she'd needed something professional to wear that wasn't scrubs, much less anything vaguely dressy, that she had no idea what had survived the move from the Lake Shore condo she and William had shared.

It was now or never. With the intention of getting up, she threw back the thin, silky sheet. Her hand bumped a strange lump in the bed.

What in the world?

Had she left all the throw pillows on the bed? She generally piled them on the chaise lounge when she drew back the covers before bed. But she'd been tired last night. Maybe she'd just tossed them aside. Her hand moved over the mound.

Firm.

Not pillows.

Her fingers traced what felt like a leg that became a hip.

Human.

Marissa shot up from the bed and stumbled as she groped at the lamp. Her heart pounded against her sternum. Light pooled across the king-size bed.

She saw the hand first.

She tilted her head and studied the familiar fingers. Long, round-tipped.

Even before her gaze swung up to the pillow and the head resting there, she knew it was William.

Lying on his side, facing her, he stared, unblinking eyes cloudy with death. *Impossible.* She squeezed her eyes shut and tried to dispel the image. Yet, when she opened her eyes once more, he was still there. The room spun around her. She shook herself. Swayed precariously before she snapped from the shock of seeing her former husband lying in her bed, obviously *dead.*

Marissa scrambled across the bed to him. Blood had puddled on the pillow behind his head and oozed down onto the sheet behind his shoulder. His dark hair was matted at the back of his neck. This could not be happening. She leaned closer to determine the source of the blood—a small hole at the base of his skull. The flesh around it was puckered and purplish. The life-giving fluid no longer seeped. Heart and pulse racing, her mind screaming at her to do something, she touched her fingers to his carotid artery.

Nothing.

Dear God, he was *dead.*

His skin was cool. Gray.

No. No. No.

He couldn't be dead. Not here. Not like this. Not possible.

She pushed him onto his back and ripped open his shirt. Buttons flew across the bed and the floor.

Pressing her cheek to his chest, she listened for a heartbeat, tried to feel his chest rise and fall.

Nothing. No heartbeat. No rush of blood.

Would CPR do anything?

She stared at his ashen skin. Cold. No pulse. Somewhere on the periphery of her consciousness, she noted the darkened area along the right side of his body where he'd been lying...*livor mortis.* The blood had pooled at the lowest point when his heart stopped beating. His eyes remained open, his unseeing gaze now fixed on the ceiling.

Feeling completely numb, she fought to summon some sort of emotional distance as she picked up his hand, felt the stiffness in his fingers and in the entire length of his arm.

He had been dead for several hours.

Trembling, she placed his hand on the sheet and scooted back to her side of the bed and off. She stood and grabbed for her cell on the table next to the bed. A quick tug pulled it loose from the power cord. She hit the three digits that would bring help.

When the dispatcher finished her spiel, Marissa spoke with remarkable calmness. "My name is Marissa Frasier." She provided her address. "My husband—ex-husband," she amended, "is dead. Please send the police."

The brief blip of calm deserted her, and Marissa collapsed onto the floor as she answered the rest of the woman's questions. Was she injured? No. What was her ex-husband's name? William Bauer. Had there been a violent encounter? No. What was the nature of the victim's injuries?

"He's been shot." The words were whispered. How could this be? She'd been sleeping in the bed right next to him.

For that matter, how had her husband been shot and ended up in her bed? Did he even have a key to this house? She had never given him one…

More questions from the dispatcher. Was she armed? No. Was there anyone else in the house? No. Wait. Her heart slammed into a frantic rhythm once more. She didn't think so. Marissa scrambled to her feet and moved slowly through the second floor of her home. She thought of the only weapon she owned. It was in the lockbox in the drawer of her bedside table. Should she go back for it?

The front doorbell sounded from downstairs and the dispatcher informed her that it was the police and emergency services; she should answer the door now. Marissa descended the stairs, disbelief swaddling her like a thick fog. Every creak of the century-old staircase echoed in her brain, seeming to ask how anyone—even William—climbed these very stairs to her room without her hearing. How had he climbed in bed next to her without her rousing?

She'd been tired, for sure. She'd slept hard. Even had a bit of a sleep hangover. Still, when they were married and working different shifts, she never failed to wake up when he came home. In college, she'd always awakened when her roommates came in—no matter how quiet they had tried to be.

As she approached the front door with its three-quarter glass panel, she realized she should have changed or grabbed a robe. Her lounge pants and tank covered her, but the fabric was thin. She suddenly felt exposed and so very cold.

Two uniformed officers stood on her stoop. The flashing lights of an ambulance sat at the curb. Another couple of uniforms hustled up the steps to join the group. This was real. William was dead…in her home.

Steadying herself, Marissa twisted the dead bolt to the unlock position and opened the door.

"Ma'am." The first man in uniform gave her a nod. "I'm Officer Jacob Tolliver. One of my fellow officers is going to stay out here on the stoop while another has a look around outside. My partner and I are coming inside to have a look around. Do you understand?"

His question warned her that she apparently appeared as much in shock as she felt. She nodded.

"Yes. He—he's in the bedroom. Second door on the left upstairs."

"You're certain there is no one else in the house?"

"Just me and…my…him, and he's dead." She tried to remember her precise steps. "I didn't check the third floor."

Officer Tolliver nodded, then he and his partner walked past her and headed for the stairs. Marissa blinked slowly as the paramedics from the ambulance came inside next. She leaned against the wall and slid down until her bottom hit the floor.

William was dead.

He'd said he was going to kill himself.

The location of the bullet hole—and she was certain that was what it was—wasn't consistent with a self-inflicted gunshot wound. She had seen her share. But, even if he had somehow managed to shoot himself in the back of the head, how did he get into her room? Into her bed?

She had no idea how much time passed before one of the officers helped her up and escorted her to the sofa.

"Dr. Frasier," he said gently, "first, is there anyone we can call for you?"

Marissa's lips parted, the reply on the tip of her tongue, but then she closed her mouth. There was no one to call. Her brother, her only living relative, was in South America with a group of doctors who were donating the next two weeks to areas with little or no available medical care.

William was dead…not that she had been able to call upon him for any sort of help in ages.

Eva…*the Colby Agency.*

"I should send a text to one of my colleagues and let her know what's happened." Dear God, she needed to call William's family.

"Why don't you let us take care of that?"

Marissa provided Eva's number to another of the officers who appeared, and he assured her he would make the call. She wasn't entirely certain why the officer preferred to make the call himself rather than have her do it. She supposed it had something to do with ensuring she didn't share the details of William's death, since there would be an investigation.

Investigation. Murder. Someone had murdered William.

Her lips trembled. This was a homicide investigation, and she was a person of interest. Her hand went to her mouth, and the urge to vomit was nearly overwhelming. Dear God.

"Dr. Frasier, can you start from the beginning and tell me what happened?"

Her mind still steeped in disbelief, she recounted all that had happened since she woke up. Twice he stopped her and urged her to take her time. The clearer the details, the better. She tried her very best to speak slowly and not leave anything out.

More people came into her home. The latest two were fully clad in disposable garb—gloves, white coveralls, matching hair covers, masks and booties. Forensic techs, she realized. They were here to collect evidence of the crime that had taken place in her home.

The shooting. The *murder.*

How in the world had William been shot right next to her without her hearing it? Wouldn't there have been a struggle?

No sooner had she finished her story to the officer than another pair of official-looking men walked in. These two wore business suits.

"Dr. Frasier," Tolliver said as he stood, "this is Detective Nader and his partner, Detective Watts. They'll be taking over from here."

The man named Nader took the chair that Tolliver vacated. Watts followed the officer up the stairs.

Marissa's throat felt dry. She wished for water or coffee. Anything.

"Let's start at the top, Dr. Frasier. I want to know everything you remember from the time you got home last night."

Marissa started at the beginning once more and told the detective the same story she'd told the officer. Nader asked her about her relationship with William. She flinched. Of course he would want to know those details. Most likely the officer simply hadn't gotten that far in his interrogation.

Because this *was* an interrogation. Not merely an interview. A man was dead.

As briefly as possible, Marissa explained her relationship with William, culminating with the recent volatile history—his words to her last night outside the ER.

Nader did a lot of scribbling.

Marissa wrung her hands together, wished again that she had a jacket or sweater and a bottle of water or a cup of coffee.

A female officer approached Nader and whispered something in his ear. The two of them glanced at Marissa.

"Give me a minute," Nader said.

The officer stepped back to the front door and waited there.

"You know a fellow named Lacon Traynor? Says he's part of your legal and security team from the Colby Agency."

Relief rushed through Marissa. "Yes." Though she didn't know the name Lacon Traynor, she absolutely knew the Colby Agency. Eva likely knew the man.

"Does the Colby Agency represent you?"

Marissa wasn't sure how to answer that question. They did, in a manner of speaking, she supposed. Though she hadn't technically met with Victoria yet and hadn't signed any documents.

But William was dead—in her bed.

She needed help.

"Yes." She hated that her voice quivered. "Yes, the Colby Agency and I are working together. Because..." She moistened her lips. "Because William's behavior was becoming increasingly erratic and threatening."

Nader sent a nod toward the waiting officer, who disappeared out the door.

"Nader!"

The shout came from the landing at the top of the stairs. Marissa's gaze moved to the man who had called out. It was the other detective, Watts.

"Yeah?" Nader glanced over his shoulder.

"Bring the doc up here for a minute, will you?"

Nader stood. "Let's have a look at your bedroom."

Marissa followed the detective to the staircase. They waited at the bottom until the two paramedics had descended.

"Coroner's on his way," one of the paramedics said to Nader.

The detective nodded and the paramedics left. Marissa watched as they, too, disappeared out her front door. Suddenly she wanted to do exactly that. She didn't want to be here any longer. She didn't want to go back upstairs. There was blood in her bed.

Bile churned in her belly.

William was dead.

Nader gestured for her to go ahead of him. Her entire body had started to shake by the time they reached her bedroom door. She hugged herself tight. It wasn't until she walked into the room this time that she smelled the stench of death. That unmistakable odor of rapidly decomposing cells, mixed with the metallic fetor of blood. The shades had been raised, filling the room with morning light. William remained on the bed. He would be there, she reminded herself, until the coroner arrived to take possession of the body.

The body. Dear God, why? Why would he do this? Yet the gunshot had been to the back of his head. He had not done this. She had to keep her thoughts straight. Her mind whirled madly. He had been murdered. She had to remember that. Someone had come into her home…

Her stomach clenched, and she suffered through another round of nausea. She had assumed that William had somehow gotten her key. But William couldn't have done this…not alone anyway.

His killer had stood over her bed…had done these awful things while she slept.

"At any time after you awakened and found your husband—"

"Ex-husband," she corrected Nader, her voice weak, practically a whisper.

He nodded. "After you discovered your dead ex-husband lying next to you, did you at any time walk to that side of the bed?"

Marissa had to think about the question for a moment, then she shook her head. "No. I scooted across the bed and pushed him onto his back." She shrugged. “All I could think was that he needed CPR, but then I realized it was too late. I suppose I was in shock.” Her hand went to her throat. “I don’t see how this could have happened.” She looked around the room. “Here. With me asleep right next to him.”

Watts held up a clear bag with a handgun inside it. “Is this .22 caliber automatic yours, Dr. Frasier?”

Marissa peered at the bag. “It looks like mine.” She gestured to her night table. “May I?”

Watts and Nader nodded. One of them muttered, “Sure.”

She moved to the table and pulled open the top drawer. A fingernail file, a brush, the book she’d started reading months ago and never gotten back to. The nail polish she never seemed to have time to use, and the lockbox. She removed it from the drawer and opened it. No weapon.

Where was her gun?

“It’s not here.” She turned back to the detective holding the weapon. “Is there a way to determine if that one is actually mine?”

She instinctively understood that the weapon in the bag, the one that was probably hers, had been used to kill William.

“Our forensic experts will make that determination,” Watts assured her.

“We’d like to swab your hands,” Nader said.

She nodded. "Of course." She had nothing to hide. Apparently she had slept through William's murder. How was that possible? Wouldn't she have heard the weapon fire? It might be small, but it was loud nonetheless. She'd fired it numerous times when she took that gun safety course. The sound would certainly have awakened her. The entire scene was sheer madness. None of this made sense.

Horror churned inside her.

Watts motioned for one of the techs to come do the honors. Marissa held her hands in front of her—they shook. The forensic tech carefully collected the samples from the skin on her hands then stepped away from her without ever making eye contact.

This was a nightmare. She squeezed her eyes shut, wondered again how this could be happening.

"We'd also like the clothes you're wearing, Dr. Frasier."

Marissa opened her eyes and met Nader's steady gaze. The female officer was there now, as well.

"Officer Holcombe will accompany you to your closet. You might want to pack a few things. I'm afraid you won't be able to come back into the house for a few days. We need time to properly process the scene."

The scene.

"Of course."

With Holcombe right behind her, Marissa went

through the en suite to the large walk-in closet that had been a key selling point for the home. Moving mechanically, she packed jeans and T-shirts and her favorite sneakers into her overnight bag. She wasn't due back to work until Tuesday. Surely they would be finished here by then. Just in case, she grabbed a set of scrubs as well as a pair of black dress slacks and a matching blouse, along with her favorite flats for meeting with Victoria Colby-Camp. She went back into the bathroom and gathered her toiletries.

Once she'd zipped the bag, Holcombe said, "I'll just need you to remove your pajamas, ma'am."

It wasn't until then that Marissa remembered she was still wearing her pj's. Rather than answer Holcombe, she returned to the closet and found another pair of jeans and a University of Illinois T-shirt. While the officer stood by, she stripped off her pj's and dropped them into the waiting bag.

"I'll need your underwear too, ma'am."

Naked save for her underwear, Marissa went back to the closet, Holcombe on her heels, and snatched another pair of panties from the drawer. She slipped off the pair she was wearing and quickly shimmied into the clean ones. While Holcombe readied the bags for turning over to one of the forensic techs, Marissa quickly dragged on the jeans and a T-shirt. She'd already packed her sneakers, so she pulled on a pair of thong sandals. With the officer waiting for her, evidence bags in hand, she abruptly remembered she would need pj's, too. She grabbed a pair and stuffed them into her bag with the rest.

With her bag hanging over her shoulder, she exited the bathroom and walked straight up to Nader. The coroner had arrived and was examining the body.

The body. It sounded so clinical. This was the man with whom she had thought she would spend the rest of her life…

"May I leave now?" She kept her gaze carefully averted from the activities across the room.

"You can." He reached into his jacket pocket and removed a business card. "Call me if you think of anything else." When she'd taken the card, he added, "I will have more questions, and there's the official statement you'll need to come downtown and make, so keep me informed of your location."

Marissa nodded and hurried from the room. She felt sick and disgusted and aggrieved. How the hell had this happened? When she went to sleep last night, her biggest concern had been how to extract William from her life. Now she had to worry about whether she was a murder suspect.

Her heart hurt for William. She would never have wished him dead.

Downstairs, yet another new arrival stood near the stone fireplace perusing the framed photographs there. This one was male and tall, with sandy blond hair. He wasn't like the others. He wore well-loved jeans, a sky blue shirt and a tan summer-weight suit jacket, but it was the cowboy boots that really set him apart from the others. He turned as she descended the last step and thrust out his hand, looking for all the world like a character from a modern-day Western movie who'd just stepped off the screen and into her living room.

"Lacon Traynor," he said, "from the Colby Agency."

Marissa took the final steps between them and accepted his hand for a quick shake. She wasn't sure what she had expected when Eva mentioned calling the Colby Agency, but this towering, cowboy-boot-wearing guy was not it. He looked vaguely familiar, but for the life of her she couldn't place him.

She finally found her voice. "Have we met?"

He gestured for her to follow him toward the kitchen. Her graystone was three stories and quite deep, but very narrow. When you walked in the front door you could see all the way out the back, with nothing but the staircase with the powder room tucked beneath it to hamper the flow. Beyond her kitchen was a set of French doors that led onto a rear deck. Beyond the deck was the small driveway. No garage, just a driveway. She was immensely grateful for something beyond street parking. A garage was on her wish list.

"We may have run into each other at the Edge when I was working with Bella and Dr. Pierce."

Now she remembered. She'd seen him once with Dr. Pierce during that awful business about his deceased wife. She remembered thinking then that this guy looked like a sheriff from a modern-day Western. Ruggedly handsome and utterly capable. She hoped he could help her the way Bella Lytle had helped Dr. Pierce, and Todd Christian had rescued Eva.

"Let's get out of here," he suggested.

She was more than ready to do that. In the kitchen, she grabbed a bottle of water from the fridge. Traynor took her bag and led the way out onto the deck and down to where her car was parked. He walked right past her vehicle and to the alley.

She followed, too overwhelmed to put up a fuss. "Where do we go from here?"

"My car. They'll want to go over yours at the lab."

Marissa hissed a disgusted sigh. They were taking over her entire life. Not that she actually minded, as long as it would help find William's killer.

A killer who had been in her home. Fear tightened around her throat.

She waited until they were seated in Traynor's car and he'd driven away before she said as much.

"Until they've collected all the evidence they believe they can find and have ruled you out as the shooter, they're going to be all over you and your property. You might as well get used to that now." He sent her a sidelong glance. "The good news is that while ruling you out, they'll also be looking for the actual perpetrator. It's no fun, but it's the way it works."

Marissa closed her eyes and leaned back against the headrest. She was so tired.

"Why don't you tell me why someone would want to make it look as if you killed your ex-husband?"

Marissa's eyes snapped open. Good God, he was right. The entire setup was about making her look responsible for William's death. But who would do that? Other than her friends at work, she had none. Her social life had fizzled out during her final years of marriage to William. He'd chased away every friend they'd ever had.

"I have no idea." Why did this have to happen now? Her life was finally headed in the direction she wanted, and this insanity had to descend upon her? What had William gotten himself into that someone would want to murder him?

"Eva filled me in on your past with Bauer. Officer Tolliver brought me up to speed on your statement, so I'm not going to make you repeat any of that for now."

Thank goodness. She'd already repeated it twice.

"Since his release from prison, have you kept up with Bauer's activities?"

"No. I tried to evict him from my life, but he still showed up every so often to antagonize me."

"So you don't know how he made money or who his associates were?"

"No." God, she'd thought she was doing the right thing distancing herself, and suddenly it felt as if all the things she didn't know were coming back to haunt her. "He sold the condo when he went to prison. Honestly, I don't even know where he lives."

Saying the words out loud made her feel all the guiltier. How could she have been married to the man for five years and not know where he was living the day he was murdered?

What kind of person did that make her?

"No worries," Traynor assured her. "We can track down all that information. But first, I'm taking you to breakfast. You need to eat."

"I'm really not hungry."

He flashed her a smile. "Maybe not, but I'm starving."

At that moment, the reality of her predicament settled fully upon her.

How in the world would she ever prove that she hadn't killed her ex-husband?

He had been murdered in her bed. The murder weapon was her gun. The security guard from the Edge could confirm that she and William had had a heated exchanged less than twenty-four hours ago.

She swung her gaze back to the man behind the wheel.

Her only hope was this cowboy who wanted to eat before they got down to business.

She was in serious trouble.

Chapter Three

Lincoln Avenue, 10:00 a.m.

Lacon had practically shoveled in the stack of pancakes he'd ordered while Dr. Frasier picked at her egg-white omelet. When she'd descended the stairs in those tight-fitting jeans and the navy university T-shirt, she'd looked like a college freshman, not the thirty-four-year-old doctor he'd been sent to protect. He'd learned a lot about her last night from Eva Bowman, fellow Colby investigator Todd Christian's soon-to-be wife. Eva and Frasier were close friends. Frasier spent an hour in the gym most every day running on the treadmill—which was different from the way she used to run through the neighborhood she loved. Her ex-husband had followed her by car several times so she'd changed her routine.

She worked hard and lived frugally to cover the mortgage for the restored graystone she'd bought when she left Bauer. She'd allowed him to keep the equity in their condo as well as the furnishings to facilitate a speedy divorce.

Between Eva and his online research, he'd learned a great deal about Dr. William Bauer, as well. Like his ex-wife, he'd graduated medical school with lower than average student loan debt because of scholarships and hard work, but the practice he'd been invited to join had not offered much in the way of fringe benefits to cover any of those loans. Frasier, on the other hand, had landed a great offer with complete coverage of any loans still outstanding. Dr. Devon Pierce, the administrator at the Edge, had given her a hefty bonus to join him when he opened the prototype advance emergency medicine facility. That bonus had served as a down payment on her new home.

While Frasier's career blossomed, Bauer's had flopped. After ferreting out all he could online about the guy, Lacon had called a friend of his who had made a career writing about life in Chicago and who kept his finger on the pulse of Chicago's streets. Since Bauer's prison stint, he sold his services as a physician to anyone who had the money to pay the exorbitant prices, and he asked no questions. He lived in a hotel and used his cell phone like an answering service.

Based on the few questions Lacon had asked her since placing their breakfast order, Frasier was completely unaware of her ex's dangerous and likely illegal activities. He'd kept the conversation fairly light in hopes she would eat. After the shock she'd suffered, she needed protein.

When she'd finally gotten down a few bites of her food and started on her second cup of coffee, Lacon decided to give her the bad news. "I did some research on Bauer."

She looked at him, her face reflecting her confusion. She had the greenest eyes. Friendly green eyes, like Eva's. And then there was that fiery red hair. He wondered if the lady had the temper to go with those wild red locks.

"You did?" She shook her head. "I'm so out of it, I didn't realize you were already looking into my situation."

"I started last night, right after I spoke to Eva."

"Oh." She looked slightly less confused now, and even a bit hopeful. "I forgot Eva called you last night." She placed her fork on the table. "I wasn't actually sure who she called. Only that it was someone from the Colby Agency."

"We would have had this discussion this morning in my boss's office except..."

She nodded. "Yeah. Except..."

"Anyway," he went on, "I discovered a number of things you probably aren't aware of. You might want to brace yourself."

The flicker of hope that had flashed in her eyes faded. "Was William in trouble?"

"Considering what happened in your bedroom, I'd say most definitely."

"What was he involved in?" She moved her hands to her lap, but not before he saw them tremble.

Now for the bad news. "He was practicing medicine as a sort of concierge doctor."

Marissa sat, obviously stunned, for a moment. "But he was only released from jail about six months ago." She shook her head. "He had patients? The state board suspended his license for unprofessional conduct. I don't understand. Had the board reviewed his case recently?"

"I don't have all the details, but I can tell you his patient list is better suited for the wanted posters on a post office wall than the files in a doctor's office."

She sat back. "I'm not sure I understand. Are you saying he was treating criminals?"

Lacon nodded. "As in, he gets a call when a drug lord or mob boss needs a bullet removed from one of his favorite henchmen."

"Oh my God." She closed her eyes in a futile effort to block the reality of what his words meant.

"My source was able to name a couple of top-of-the-food-chain thugs he's done work for. They were paying him big bucks for the work and for his silence."

She allowed this news to sink in before asking, "So whoever came into my home last night and killed

William may have been hired by an actual drug lord or mob boss?"

"That would be my guess."

All those soft curls swished as she shook her head. "Then why not kill me, too? What if I had suddenly awakened in the middle of what they were doing? Or if my neighbor heard the gunshot?"

"From what you described and what Officer Tolliver told me, this was a professional hit. Bauer stepped on someone's toes, and they showed him who was boss. Why they chose your place to carry this out, no clue just yet. If the shooter used your gun, my guess is the police will find a pillow or something along those lines that was used to muffle the sound."

Her face clouded with worry. "I hadn't thought of that. Still, I'm not a heavy sleeper. I can't believe I slept through someone coming into my home and killing my husband right next to me."

Lacon was having trouble with that one, as well. "While I waited for you to come back downstairs, I noticed there was a half-empty bottle of wine on the counter in your kitchen. Did you have wine last night?"

"Yes. I had one glass. I told the detective as much."

"Anything unusual about how you felt after you drank the wine or when you woke up? Groggy? Headache?"

"I remember I felt really tired last night, but that's not unusual. I work long, hectic hours at the ER. So

I went straight to bed after the wine. This morning, I did feel a little sluggish, had a mild headache, but I assumed it was about finding William dead next to me. I told this to the detective, too."

"They're probably drawing the same picture I am, Dr. Frasier. Most likely they'll have the wine tested for drugs. It might be best if you had a blood test to see if there's anything we need to know about."

"We can stop by the Edge."

"From there we'll go to the safe house and get you settled. We can start going over what we know and what we don't from there. We've already got people gathering more accurate and detailed information about your ex-husband's activities since his release. It won't take us long to figure this out."

"Safe house?"

"The police won't release your home for a day or two, and it's best that we keep you out of reach of whatever trouble Bauer found himself in until we determine the source and any potential threat to you. You don't need to worry. We've got you covered."

The first hint of a smile tilted her lips. "Thank you."

Colby Safe House, 1:30 p.m.

WHEN MARISSA HEARD the words *safe house*, she hadn't expected a fortress. The house sat in the woods on the edge of Lake Michigan, a good forty-five minutes from downtown Chicago. A towering brick wall surrounded the property on all sides save the one facing the lake. Enormous iron gates had opened for their entrance onto the property and immediately closed behind them. If not for the large windows, the house would have looked more like a stone prison than a mere house. Lush flowers and shrubs bordered the stone facade, softening it a bit.

Traynor parked his car in front of the house. He gazed up at it. "State-of-the-art security system operated by keypad or voice control. Steel shutters can be closed over all the windows and doors. No one can touch you here."

For some reason, she didn't feel the slightest bit better about this nightmare. Part of her held on to the fleeting possibility that any moment she would wake up and discover that the whole morning had been a dream. Things like this didn't happen to regular, everyday people. She felt as if she'd been shoved onto the set of a thriller movie. Any minute now the director would give the order to run.

Traynor climbed out of the car and rounded the hood to her side. She emerged to join him. She shook off the troubling thoughts and focused on the reality staring her in the face right this second. She was standing in front of a safe house. A place where she would stay until William's murder was all sorted out.

"It's beautiful, in a sort of austere way," she said, mostly to make conversation.

"You'll feel more comfortable inside."

At the door, he pressed his palm onto a keypad and the door locks released. He pushed the door open and waited for her to step inside before him. The walls were a warm beige with lovely gloss white trim. Rich furnishings and draperies added a very elegant touch. All those large windows allowed sun to pour in between the slats of the shutters. Unlike the exterior, inside it actually felt warm and inviting.

"You're right. It's a very lovely house."

"Take whatever room you'd like upstairs, and then join me for coffee in the kitchen."

She took her bag from him and headed for the grand staircase. Upstairs, she wandered into the first room with a view of the rear gardens and the lake. The rock paths and dense greenery made the stone patio and gorgeous pool with its rushing waterfall look as if they had always been there—as if they were part of the natural landscape. She sighed. Too bad this wasn't some exotic resort where she'd spend the next few days soaking up the sun. She hadn't taken a vacation in years.

But this was no vacation.

Feeling more exhausted than she had since medical school, she tossed her bag onto a chair and opened it. One by one she hung her jeans and T-shirts in the largest closet she'd ever seen. Maybe hanging them would help with the wrinkles from being stuffed into her bag. She carried her toiletries to the massive en suite. A luxurious marble tub, a shower for at least four and two sinks designed in colorful glass that crowned the endless vanity. The window over the tub looked out over the lake, as well. The view put the bathroom over the top.

"A grand hideaway," she mumbled.

She leaned against the counter and stared at her reflection. Her pale skin looked even paler. The dark circles under her eyes spoke loudly of the morning's horrors. The stop they'd made at the Edge had taken longer than she'd anticipated. Eva insisted on knowing exactly what happened. She drew the necessary blood samples and ensured them the analysis would be handled stat.

Eva had promised to explain everything to Dr. Pierce. As much as she adored Eva, Marissa really hadn't wanted to talk about it anymore to anyone except those involved directly in the investigation. Her body and soul felt tender, and she needed time to think and process all that had happened. But sweet Eva had coaxed the story out of her. In the end, Marissa supposed it was better if her dearest friend, as well as Dr. Pierce, understood the precarious situation.

She supposed *precarious* was the best way to describe her current dilemma. Part of her wanted to call her brother, but he would only insist on coming home, and that wouldn't be fair. He was doing important work. She doubted this was going away anytime soon. There was always time to call her brother later if the situation deteriorated.

Pushing away from the vanity, she trudged back into the bedroom. She made it as far as the bed before she collapsed. Traynor was waiting for her downstairs, but she couldn't seem to make her body obey the command to get up and move.

Tears rushed over her lashes and down her cheeks. She didn't want to cry. It was too late for tears, but she couldn't stop them. Giving up the fight, she dropped her face into her hands and let them come. Her shoulders shook with the sobs that tore at her heart. No matter that she and William had been over for years—she had loved him so deeply before everything fell apart. She had expected to spend the rest of her life with him…to have children with him. Eventually. Though she couldn't say that she still loved him, she cared about him and wanted the best for him.

Now he was dead.

He'd threatened to kill himself and her mere hours before his death, and somehow that made the tragedy all the sadder. Had he really wished her dead? She'd tried so hard to help him before his abuse turned physical. She had already stayed in the marriage too long. Why was it women so often stayed, somehow believing they could salvage what remained of their marriage?

Foolish. Simply foolish.

A soft knock on the door drew her attention there. Traynor stood in the doorway, his tall frame and broad shoulders filling the space. She swiped at her eyes and attempted to pull herself together. "You'll have to excuse me. I don't know what's wrong with me. I can't stop crying."

Most men usually found an immediate excuse to disappear when a woman cried. To her surprise, Lacon Traynor crossed the room, grabbed the box of tissues on the bedside table and sat down on the bed next to her.

"You needed to cry," he said gently as he offered her a couple of tissues. "It doesn't help to keep all the emotions bottled up inside. This has been a seriously bad day for you. If anyone I've ever met needed a good cry, it's you."

She dabbed at her eyes and nose. "I keep asking myself how it happened without me waking up. No matter how I examine it, it doesn't make sense."

"We'll have a better handle on things when the lab results are in. For now, just know that none of it was your fault. You're a victim in this."

Marissa stared at the soggy tissue in her hand and asked the question that had been pounding in her brain since Traynor told her what he'd discovered about William. "Why do you think they didn't kill me?" She shrugged. "I mean, I can see how, if William was lurking around my house and they followed him there, it was a coincidence of sorts. But it feels like more than just a coincidence."

"The body was staged," Traynor said. "Since there was no sign of a struggle in your home, I believe they drugged Bauer and put him in position, then shot him."

Marissa shuddered. She'd seen enough gunshot wounds involving .22s to know that when dealing with a caliber that small, all kinds of things could go awry. The bullet could have glanced off his skull, traveled around beneath the skin and come out someplace else. The damned thing could have ended up hitting her. After all, William had been lying on the bed facing her.

But that wasn't what happened. The coroner's report would tell the detailed story, but shoving the muzzle against the back of his neck just below the base of the skull in that particular spot pretty much guaranteed the brain stem would be damaged. The likelihood of death was extremely high. Since there had been no exit wound, the bullet no doubt penetrated the skull and bounced around in the brain, doing all manner of additional damage. Even if by some twist of fate William had lived, he would in all probability have suffered significant physical and cognitive damage.

She pushed away the thoughts. If he'd been drugged, perhaps he hadn't suffered. She hoped he hadn't suffered. As horribly as he'd treated her in recent years, he hadn't deserved to be murdered.

"Were they trying to send me a message for some reason?" Marissa couldn't see the thought process behind such a move. She had nothing to do with William's work or any debts he might owe to angry loan sharks. Frankly, she hardly knew the man who had once been her husband anymore.

Traynor didn't answer for a second that turned into five. "That's it, isn't it?" She stared directly at his face, silently demanding that he meet her gaze. "You believe the person or persons who did this wanted me to know they could come into my home and commit murder right in my most intimate space. They left me alive for some reason, didn't they?"

"That's one of the theories, yes. Are you certain you're not aware of any activities Bauer was involved in? Could he have given you something to keep for him? Something they might want?"

"No. After I landed in the hospital from the beating he gave me, I cut all ties with him. The only times I've seen him since his trial are when he has shown up unexpectedly on the street outside my house or in the parking lot at the market where I shop. He's called and left messages, but I never answer them. Eventually I changed my number. I never allowed him into my new house. When he came to the ER yesterday, that was the first time he'd come to my work."

"If they believe you have something that belongs to them or something they want," Traynor offered, "we'll know soon enough."

She drew in a deep breath and squared her shoulders. "I think I need a walk."

"Come on." He stood. "I'll show you around the property."

Downstairs, he took her on a tour of the kitchen, which was huge and filled with gleaming cabinetry and sleek countertops. The appliances were commercial, restaurant-style pieces of art with enough bells and whistles to make any chef happy. A dream kitchen by anyone's standards. Traynor's next stop was the gym. The array of equipment would satisfy the most hardcore workout enthusiast. Marissa would spend some time here for sure. Next to the gym was the garage that housed six luxury vehicles; some were even bulletproof. She had to admit, she was impressed.

Back through the kitchen and the dining room was a den at the back of the house. A floor-to-ceiling fireplace sat against one wall; big comfy furniture filled the center of the room, and a sizable television was tucked into a discreet nook. But the part that stole Marissa's attention was the wall of French doors and windows that zoomed all the way to the vaulted ceiling to allow as much of the lake view into the room as possible. She could live in this one room.

Outside, the breeze coming off the water chased

away the afternoon heat. They followed the stone path, and Traynor pointed out the boat dock and the helipad. The safe house was prepared with a number of escape routes, as well as a safe room that could withstand just about any sort of attack.

"When did you join the Colby Agency?" She leaned against the steel railing that topped the seawall at the back of the property. The air was crisp and fresh, and she felt herself starting to relax.

"Six years ago." He propped his arms on the railing and stared out at the water. "Before that I was a bounty hunter."

Marissa smiled. No surprise there. She'd had him pegged as a rugged law enforcement type. "Where did you grow up?"

"Floresville, Texas," he announced proudly. "Half an hour south of San Antonio. The family ranch is there. I have two brothers and a sister who run the family business, one of the biggest cattle operations in the state. My dad's retired now, but he still gives his input."

She gazed out over the water for a moment before searching his face. "You didn't want to stay with the family business?"

He smiled, and the expression startled her. Lacon Traynor was an attractive man, but when he smiled it was a genuinely beautiful sight. She liked his smile. His eyes, too. He had those light brown, almost golden eyes. The blond hair and gold eyes were a vivid contrast to his tanned skin.

Her detailed analysis of his physical assets puzzled her. It didn't seem appropriate to admire the man's attributes after what had happened. Honestly, she couldn't even remember the last time she'd paid attention to whether a man was attractive or not, much less noticed his smile or his eyes. Something inside her had shut off all those feelings after William threw her up against the wall a few times and then tossed her down the stairs. It really was a miracle she'd survived without truly devastating injuries.

But no matter that he had done that awful thing to her, she still never wished him dead.

Yet he was dead, and somehow even in death he'd found a way to punish her for being a better doctor than he could be...for working harder than he ever considered working. And for trying to do the right thing when he no longer cared.

She had a right to be happy, and William—alive or dead—had no right to try to take that happiness from her. Anger sparked deep inside her.

"I was far too cocky and too full of myself to be happy on the ranch. I needed adventure. For a long time—" his gaze drifted back to the water "—rounding up the bad guys and bringing them in was enough. But then a really bad one got out of jail after a two-year stint, and went back home and killed his ex-wife. I saw things differently after that. Doing the job no longer held the same appeal. I needed distance and a fresh start."

"The ex-wife was someone you knew?" She had a terrible feeling the story didn't end with a job going wrong. His words carried the weight of far more than mere facts or statistics. This was personal.

"She was my fiancée. We were getting married the next month. He killed her just to get back at me for hauling his sorry ass to San Antonio to stand trial the first time."

"I'm so sorry."

He nodded, stared down at his hands. "I was out of town when he was released, a week earlier than expected. I had a bail jumper to pick up in El Paso. The local cops took care of the bastard though. He made the mistake of trying to fight back when they cornered him, and they took him out."

"So you moved away." She didn't blame him.

"I needed a change of scenery."

"The winters are very different here," she commented, easing the topic of conversation away from his painful past.

"You're not kidding. But I wanted to work for the best. It was important to me to find work that allowed me to help people before the worst happened. The Colby Agency gave me that opportunity." He sent her another smile, this one considerably dimmer than the first. "Most of the time anyway."

"Sometimes there's just no way to see what's coming." Not in a million years would she have suspected William of this behavior. She'd had no idea his fall from grace had taken him so far down.

Lacon placed one of his broad palms over her hand on the railing and gave it a reassuring squeeze. "We'll figure this out."

His promise warmed her. Her cell vibrated against her hip, shattering the moment of encouragement. She pulled it from her pocket and checked the screen, expecting it to be Eva or one of the detectives. Blocked Call flashed on the screen. "Marissa Frasier."

"Hello, Dr. Frasier."

The deep voice was male, but not one she recognized. She hesitated, waiting for the man to go on.

"You have a very lovely home. I sincerely apologize that my business with your husband caused you any inconvenience."

Fear rushed over her, and she instinctively grabbed Traynor's arm. "Who is this?"

"You'll know soon enough," the man promised. "For now, I need your help. You see, your husband left me in a very difficult situation. Now you're going to have to pick up his slack."

"I have no idea what you're talking about," she argued. Traynor's head was next to hers now so he could hear, as well. "William and I divorced a long time ago. Whatever business he had with you has nothing to do with me."

"You are a doctor, are you not?"

She didn't answer. She didn't need to, because he already knew.

"Yes, I know you are. Your late husband bragged about you quite often. He still kept photos of you in his phone. You're still listed as *wife* in his cell phone. How does that make you feel, Dr. Frasier?"

The bastard had William's phone. The police had asked her about his phone. The news about the photos and the way she was listed in William's phone sent a strangely unnerving sensation chasing along her spine. She wasn't sure how she was supposed to feel about that announcement. Maybe William simply hadn't taken the time to clear the past from his phone. Now she would never know. *Didn't matter.*

"What do you want?" she demanded.

"Drive into the city, Dr. Frasier. When you reach Division Street, I will send you the address you need to find. Involve the police, and you will regret it. Refuse to come, and you will regret it."

"Why would I do this when you won't tell me who you are?"

Her phone vibrated, making her heart skip another beat.

"Have a look at the photo you just received," he said as if he, too, had felt the vibration.

She drew her phone from her ear and touched the screen to open the text message. A photo of Jeremiah Owens wearing his blue cast appeared on the screen. It was obvious the photo had been taken as he and his mother exited the ER earlier last evening.

"Did you receive the photo?" the man asked.

Marissa didn't have to question why he sent it. The realization sat like a boulder on her chest. "Yes."

"Your late husband told me how much you love your patients. I'm certain you will want to ensure little Jeremiah remains safe, no matter the cost or the inconvenience."

Fury overrode all logic. "I don't know what sort of game—"

"This is not a game, Dr. Frasier. You will do exactly as I say. Any supplies you require will be provided by my associates. Do not notify the police. Trust me, I have eyes and ears everywhere in this city. Do not make a mistake, or little Jeremiah's mother will be burying her son while you stand by and wonder why you didn't listen more carefully to my instructions. I'm certain you do not want that to happen."

The fury drained instantly, leaving only the fear. Her heart hammered so hard she could scarcely manage a breath. "It'll take me nearly an hour to get back to the city."

"I'm counting on you, Dr. Frasier. Respond to the text I sent to let me know when you have arrived at Division. Instructions will follow."

The call ended.

She lifted her gaze to Traynor's. "I have to go. I

don't know who this man is or what he expects from me, but I have to go."

"No." He took her hand. "*We* have to go."

Chapter Four

"You need to drive faster."

Lacon couldn't remember the last time anyone had asked him to drive faster. "I'm running ten miles an hour over the speed limit now, Dr. Frasier. We don't want to risk a traffic stop."

Frasier twisted around in her seat and stared out the back window, then did the same on the passenger side. She stretched across the console and checked behind him and then in front of him to see his side of the highway. "I don't see any cops. Please, you need to hurry."

"Try to calm down," he urged. Hell, she was making him nervous. He got it. She was a doctor, and this wasn't part of her daily routine. He'd probably pass out if he had to cut open a patient and poke around their organs. "Bella will be patching through the conference call any second now. We need to keep our heads on straight until we get a better handle on the situation."

"Bella Lytle?"

"The one and only." Bella was soon to be Bella Pierce. Dr. Devon Pierce, the Edge administrator, had already popped the question. "She's coordinating a call between us, Victoria and Chicago PD."

"What?" Frasier glared at him. "He said no police! He claimed to have eyes and ears in the department."

Had she not been listening when he called Victoria? "Victoria and Lucas know the police department inside out. They won't be calling Nader or Watts. Whoever they work with will be someone completely trustworthy. Their connections go well above any possible leaks."

"Oh, my God." Frasier hugged herself. "If something happens to that child..."

Lacon made the next turn. "He wants you scared, Marissa." He used her first name in hopes of getting her full attention. "Men like him—whoever the hell he is—use fear as a means to gain power. Don't give him the power."

She stared at the cell phone clutched in her hand, the picture of the little boy on the screen. "Mrs. Owens doesn't have any other children, and she can't have any more. Her husband was killed in a construction accident two years ago." She held up the phone, aiming the screen at Lacon. "This child is all she has. I can't risk taking him away from her, do you understand?"

"I do understand." He pressed a little harder on

the accelerator, adding another five miles per hour to his speed. "I will do everything I can to make sure nothing happens to the child or to you."

His cell rang, the call coming over the speaker system in the car. He'd set it that way so they could both hear the conversation and respond as needed.

He touched the screen. "Traynor here. I have you on speaker so Dr. Frasier can hear you, as well."

"Dr. Frasier, this is Victoria Colby-Camp. On the line with me are Lucas Camp, Ian Michaels, Bella Lytle—all from the Colby Agency. From Chicago PD's Bureau of Detectives we have Chief Connie Staten. We also have Chief Anthony Waller, who commands the Bureau of Organized Crime since, based on what we've learned about the late Dr. Bauer, we feel we're dealing with an element of organized crime."

"Have you learned something new about William?"

Frasier's voice sounded small and weary. Lacon hated not being able to take the weight of this fear off her shoulders. Before Victoria or the others could respond, he interjected, "I've brought her up to speed on what we had as of this morning."

"Dr. Frasier, this is Chief Waller. We had been watching Dr. Bauer for about two months. We have reason to believe he was deeply involved with Vito Anastasia. To give you a quick overview of our position, in recent decades we've made great strides in eliminating the mob element in Chicago. It still exists, but nothing like it did thirty years ago. Anastasia is doing all within his power to give rise to a new group called the Network. In the last year we've seen a startling increase in homicides and all manner of organized crime. We believe Anastasia is behind that deadly increase. Our goal is to take him down as quickly as possible but, as you are aware, I'm sure, we need evidence against him for that. We could use your help toward that end."

"We will not allow you to use our client in any way that will endanger her life," Victoria stated, her tone professional but firm.

Lacon was grateful his boss had spoken up. He'd been struggling to hold back that same warning. He had been with the Colby Agency long enough to know Victoria's feelings on the subject.

"Ms. Colby-Camp—" a female voice joined the conversation "—this is Chief Staten. You have my word that we would never allow an operation that would endanger Dr. Frasier's life. We're only asking that she share information with us. The fact of the matter is she's already in Anastasia's crosshairs. Whatever his goal, he will not stop until he accomplishes that goal. If anything, we can help protect her."

"How was William—Dr. Bauer involved?" Frasier demanded.

Lacon glanced at her, wished he could give her arm a squeeze of reassurance, but at this speed he needed both hands on the wheel. He had a bad feeling about this. With people this high up the department food chain involved, Bauer had been more than just involved with Vito Anastasia. Lacon would bet everything he owned that he had been caught by the department and forced to feed them info—acting as a confidential informant. Why else would Anastasia assassinate his doctor? He hadn't said as much to Frasier, but the murder was a blatant assassination. The mob executed their people when they stole from them and when they ratted them out. Bauer had done one or the other, no question.

"As a doctor, you're aware that all gunshot victims are reported. Anytime a known criminal shows up in an ER, if he's recognized, he's reported. To avoid those types of situations and to keep his family and crew healthy, a man like Anastasia hires a doctor to take care of things discreetly. Dr. Bauer had been working for Anastasia in that capacity for five months."

Lacon noticed the way Frasier's hand trembled as she covered her mouth. This was not the man she'd known, the man she'd loved. By the time he was murdered, Bauer had been a stranger. A stranger who had dragged her into a world so vile and so dangerous that she couldn't possibly comprehend the risk involved with merely being on the bastard's radar.

"What level of cooperation are you looking for?" Victoria asked the question blazing in Lacon's brain.

"For now, see what Anastasia wants," Waller said. "If it turns out he wants Dr. Frasier to assume the position left open by Dr. Bauer, then we would want her to take it for a period of time and feed intelligence to us."

Lacon couldn't help it—he laughed. "Why don't you just ask her to put a gun to her head and pull the trigger? The result would be basically the same."

That Victoria didn't caution him to back off spoke volumes. She agreed. The proposal was unreasonable.

The two cops on the call started talking at once, arguing why it made complete sense. Victoria countered their denials, backing Lacon's concerns.

"I can't make any promises right now," Frasier spoke up, her voice loud and firm this time. "All I care about at the moment is making sure Jeremiah Owens is safe. Unless you can do that, we have nothing else to talk about at this time."

Lacon smiled to himself. *Way to go, doc.*

"We have undercover surveillance on the Owens home. Mother and son are both inside," Staten assured her.

Frasier shared a look with Lacon. He knew what she was thinking. "Whatever you do," he warned the representatives of the department on the line, "under no circumstances can Anastasia discover that we've contacted you, so those boots you have on the ground better be damned careful."

"I am confident Chiefs Staten and Waller will

not allow that to happen," Victoria said, echoing his warning a tad more diplomatically.

The two chiefs gave their assurances that the operation was locked down tight, and the call ended with one final urge from Victoria for Frasier to be careful.

Lacon's phone immediately rang again. This time it was only Victoria. She reminded him that his sole obligation was to Dr. Frasier and keeping her safe. Frasier thanked her.

When they reached Division Street, Lacon parked at a gas station on the corner of West Division Street and North Winchester Avenue. "Send the text."

Frasier held his gaze for several seconds before typing, I'm at Division.

Half a minute, maybe more, elapsed and a soft ping announced a response. Corner of 1735 West Hubbard St. at intersection of Hermitage Ave.

Frasier showed him the screen. Lacon nodded. "I know the area."

Five turns and hardly more than five minutes later, they pulled up in front of a warehouse for lease. Tension rippled through his muscles. Lacon shifted into Park and turned to face her. "Stay close to me. No matter what else happens, stick to me like glue. I do not want you out of my sight for any reason. Got it?"

"Got it." She swallowed hard, the muscles of her

throat working. "How will your people know where we are?"

"Every Colby investigator has a tracking device installed in their personal vehicle. The same goes for my phone. Just remember, no matter what else happens, we cannot be separated."

She nodded. "Wait. What's my excuse for having you with me?"

Her voice trembled, and he wished he knew the words to say that would ease her fears, but there were none. "Your ex had been threatening you. You hired personal security through a private firm. I'm your bodyguard."

She nodded. "Good. Okay."

"I'll get out first and open your door."

She moistened her lips. "Make it look real. Right."

"Make it look real," he agreed.

Lacon cleared her fear from his head and reached for the door handle. He emerged from the car and scanned the street in both directions. No traffic. Only a parked car here and there. He walked around to the passenger side and opened the door, again surveying the area. As soon as she was out of the car, he ushered her to the front entrance of the building marked 1735.

"Stay behind me," he said before opening the door.

She nodded. He grasped the knob, gave it a twist and pushed the door inward. She stuck close behind him just like he'd instructed.

Lights were on, but the place looked deserted other than a few stacks of shipping crates. As soon as the door closed behind them, four armed men materialized from behind the crates and fanned out in a circle around them. All four were dressed in black suits, black shirts and full-face masks, also black. One skirted around them until he was behind Lacon and started the expected pat-down. His weapon was removed from his side holster.

Taking a step forward, putting her side by side with him, Frasier said, "I'm Dr. Marissa Frasier. Your boss is expecting me."

The tallest of the four walked toward them until he stood toe-to-toe with Lacon. "You were instructed to come alone." He stabbed the muzzle of his .44 caliber automatic against Lacon's forehead. "Now I have to take care of this excess baggage."

"If you kill him," Frasier said, her voice strangely calm, "I won't do whatever it is your boss called me here to do."

As much as Lacon appreciated her support, he did not want her to be a hero.

The man in front of Lacon, who appeared to be in charge, turned his head toward her. "Then I'll have to kill you, too, and the boss will be most unhappy."

Frasier took a step toward the man. Lacon gritted his teeth. He had to hold himself back from grabbing her. Three weapons shifted their aims toward her head. She ignored them and stared directly at the man in front of Lacon. "Then you might as well do what you have to. This is my personal bodyguard, and wherever I go, he goes. Are we clear?"

Lacon held his breath, prayed she hadn't just signed her death warrant.

The thug in front of him pressed the fingers of his free hand to his ear, touching the earpiece he wore. The boss was listening, and he had made a decision.

Let it be the one we need.

"Let's go," the man in charge announced. He stepped aside and gestured for Lacon and Frasier to precede him.

Lacon was able to breathe again. He leaned toward her. "Do not do that again."

She ignored him the same way she had the other guy. Maybe the doctor was a lot tougher than she looked.

Thug number two walked beside Lacon, and the others walked behind them. The procession continued into a corridor behind the large space they had entered. Three doors down on the left another man, dressed all in black like his friends, opened a door and stepped aside for them to enter.

Frasier was ushered into the room first. Lacon stayed right behind her. In the center of the room, beneath the fluorescent light that flickered incessantly, a man lay on a white sheet that looked much like a drop cloth used for painting. His hands were tied in front of him and his feet were secured at the ankles. Blood soaked his shirt. The gag in his mouth prevented him from speaking, but he made frantic sounds as they approached.

Next to the man on the floor was an open box loaded with what looked like medical supplies. Lacon didn't need a map or a block of instruction to see where this was going. Along with the medical supplies, spread out on the floor were a number of torture devices. A battery and jumper cables for delivering shocks. Dental forceps for extracting teeth. And an array of other nasty tools for generating pain.

The thug in charge answered a call on his cell. He made a couple of agreeable sounds and then set the phone to speaker.

"Dr. Frasier, I need this man alive," the voice of their caller—the one they suspected was Vito Anastasia—announced. "Your survival depends completely on his. Do not let me down, or this is where the police will find your body."

Frasier charged forward and dropped onto her knees next to the man. She surveyed his injuries. Lacon moved closer to her, but the Top Thug pulled him back. Lacon stared him dead in the eyes. Hoped like hell he got the chance to kick his ass.

"I may need his assistance," Frasier said.

Top Thug pushed Lacon toward her. "He's all yours."

Lacon crouched next to Frasier. "What can I do?"

She poked around in the box, surveying the supplies. "First, I need to sedate him." She picked up a bottle and a syringe.

"No!" Top Thug snarled. "We need him conscious."

"I cannot remove the bullet while he is conscious," Frasier snapped. She gestured to another drug bottle. "We'll wake him up when I'm done."

Top Thug stepped back.

Damn, Lacon was impressed. The doc was holding her own with these dirtbags.

Frasier cleaned her hands and forearms with an antibacterial solution before donning a pair of gloves. Lacon removed his jacket and did the same. When she had everything she needed spread on a white towel that the instruments had been wrapped in, she moved closer to the injured man and began her work. She checked his vitals and then ripped open his shirt to get a closer look at the injury.

Tears ran from the guy's eyes. He'd wet himself. Frasier spoke quietly to him as she worked. "I'm going to give you morphine. You won't feel any of this."

While she attended to the man, Lacon committed his face and physical features to memory. Whoever he was, he'd pissed off Anastasia or had information he wanted. Lacon considered how they might be able to help him, but not a single idea came to mind that wouldn't get one or both of them killed.

When the man had lost consciousness, she removed the rag stuffed in his mouth. To Lacon she said, "I want you to keep an eye on his blood pressure."

He grabbed the blood pressure cuff she had removed from his left arm and moved to the other side so he wouldn't be in her way. He strapped the cuff into place and pressed the button to start the process. Luckily for him, this particular monitor did all the work.

"About the same, one-ten over seventy."

Frasier nodded and continued cleaning the area around the injury. Her moves were so precise and so rhythmic, Lacon found himself mesmerized by the steady, quick steps. She opened the entrance wound a little wider, had the bullet out in a few precise moves and began closing the wound in a matter of minutes. Lacon checked the guy's blood pressure periodically. Thankfully it stayed fairly consistent.

When she had dressed the wound and peeled off her gloves, the top thug said, "Wake him up."

Frasier pushed to her feet and turned to him. "First, I didn't see any additional bleeding, but I can't be certain there isn't damage I couldn't see. He needs an ultrasound and other tests to determine if there are additional internal injuries. This is not a sterile environment. He'll need an antibiotic, and I still can't say that he'll get through this without a serious infection."

Top Thug shook his head. "Doesn't matter. Just wake him up and then you can go."

Lacon removed the cuff and slowly stood, careful not to make any sudden moves. These guys wanted the man awake and patched up so they could continue torturing him for information. The last thing they wanted was for him to die without divulging his secrets. Damn.

"He should be in a hospital," Frasier argued.

"Wake him up," the thug ordered, the muzzle of his weapon nudging her in the chest.

When she didn't make a move to do so, his cohort stuck his weapon in Lacon's face. He didn't flinch, but his gut sure as hell clenched.

"Wake him up or your bodyguard dies," Top Thug warned.

Frasier trembled visibly. She glared at the piece of shit a moment longer before crouching next to the box of supplies and preparing a shot of Narcan. Seconds after she administered the injection, the man's eyes opened.

Top Thug yanked her to her feet. "Now go, or watch your friend die."

She started to argue, but Lacon took her by the

arm and ushered her out of the room. Two of the thugs followed them out of the building; one returned Traynor's weapon. She kept looking back, and he kept pushing her forward. They had to get out of here or they could end up dead, too.

Damn. Damn. Damn.

He ushered her into the car, fastened her seat belt and then closed her door. When he dropped behind the wheel, he started the car and drove away immediately, his pulse throbbing. Son of a bitch!

They were leaving that guy to die.

And if they warned the police, Anastasia would know.

There had to be something he could do to stop this travesty.

Then the answer hit him square between the eyes. He called 911.

Frasier stared at him, her eyes wide with fear. "What're you doing?"

When the dispatcher had finished his spiel, Lacon said, "Man, you gotta get the fire department to 1735 West Hubbard. Smoke is boiling outta that old warehouse. I think some homeless people are living in there. Hurry!" He ended the call.

He glanced at Frasier. Her green eyes filled with tears, and a barely perceptible smile tugged at her lips. "Thank you."

And then she broke down and cried.

Lacon reached across the console and took her hand in his.

Chapter Five

Colby Safe House, 7:30 p.m.

Marissa pulled on her pj's. The lavender bottoms and white tank top with its matching lavender phrase, Doctors Are People Too, were badly wrinkled from being stuffed carelessly into the bag. Didn't matter. She stared at her reflection, images of the gunshot victim she'd patched up—the man whose name she didn't know—flashing over and over in her head.

She hoped the fire department had arrived before the bastards in the masks could finish him off. No matter that she understood doing anything further to help him was impossible given the situation, she still ached at the idea that she and Traynor had walked out of that damned warehouse and left the wounded man there. She had taken an oath to heal…not to walk away and leave someone injured on the floor.

Despite thinking she was all cried out, more tears flowed down her cheeks as she thought of the call she'd had to make to William's parents. Though they had stopped speaking to her after the trial, she still felt their anguish. William's death was such an immense waste. He was still so young. Eventually he might very well have been able to pull his life back together. William had obviously been desperate; otherwise he would never have resorted to such unexpected criminal behavior.

But the decision had been his alone. Some part of her felt the weight of guilt, but it was not her fault. Intellectually, she understood that irrefutable fact. On an emotional level, it was a different story. She had loved him. They had lived as husband and wife for five years. She had wanted to see the good in him even when he'd stood outside the ER and told her he intended to kill her. She hadn't wanted to believe he'd meant it.

Had that been his warped way of warning her something bad was about to happen? Had he thought such a threat would prompt her to go to the police? She would likely never know.

Men like Vito Anastasia cared nothing for human life—only about what they could take. She wasn't naive. She watched the news, but she had never been forced to bear witness to that cold, harsh reality until today. The sick and injured came to her, inside the safety of the ER. She wasn't out there witnessing the atrocities that occurred far too often on the streets of most cities. She'd certainly never walked away knowing somebody she'd provided care for would surely be murdered in the hours to follow.

Was what she'd done any different from treating a gunshot victim in the ER who ended up right back on the street hours or days later to dive into the same life of crime that had put a bullet in him in the first place? Where did her obligation end and that of the police begin? Or the patient, for that matter?

Her arms went around her body and attempted to stop the trembling. Had Traynor not hauled her out of that warehouse and she'd stayed, what could she have done to stop four armed thugs? Nothing.

There was no going back. At this point, she just needed to know the fire department had arrived in time.

Her damp curls tucked into a hair clip, she emerged from her room and went in search of Traynor. Some errant brain cell reminded her that she needed to eat. It had been many hours since she'd forced herself to swallow a few bites of the omelet. But her stomach didn't feel capable of accepting food. Her throat felt so dry and constricted, she wasn't sure she could swallow even a tiny bite.

You need the energy to keep going. That much was true.

Downstairs she found Traynor making sandwiches. "I was just about to come find you." He set a plate on the counter in front of her. "Ham and cheese. I didn't know if you wanted mayo or mustard."

Her stomach rumbled and knotted at the same time. She pushed into place what she hoped passed for a smile. "Thank you."

"Whatever you want to drink, you'll probably find in the fridge." He placed the second piece of bread atop his own sandwich. "They keep this place stocked like a five-star resort. Make yourself at home."

She put a hand to her mouth, then allowed it to slide down her throat. "I'm not sure I can eat."

He lifted his sandwich. "Try it. You'll probably be surprised how hungry you are after you get down the first couple of bites."

Maybe he was right. Before she dared try, she wandered to the fridge and grabbed a bottle of cold water. She downed a long swallow, her throat immediately feeling better. He picked up her plate as well as his own and moved to the table. She followed, too tired and too overwhelmed to do much else.

Hoping she could actually swallow something more than water, she took a bite of the sandwich.

"This is hard for you," he said. "You're accustomed to a clinical environment where the variables, though at times outside your control, are a different kind of battle. Everyone in the room is generally attempting to help the patient, not cause harm. It doesn't work that way in the environment set up by a guy like Anastasia."

She closed her eyes for a moment and tried her

best not to sound as angry and bitter as she felt. “I watch the news, Mr. Traynor. I’m well aware how the world works.”

“But you don’t usually find yourself caught in the middle of the lead story. This is a whole different world. The people who end up in front of you want help, and there’s rarely anyone trying to prevent you from providing the necessary help.”

“True,” she said wearily, “unless you count insurance companies.”

He laughed and she couldn’t help smiling, even if it hurt her face to do so.

“Have you heard if the man in the warehouse made it?” She held her breath as she waited for his answer. Whatever the man was guilty of, she wanted him to be alive. Deep down, she understood that she was likely kidding herself. Men like Anastasia wouldn’t leave those sorts of loose ends.

Why in the world would William have risked working for a man like Anastasia?

Guilt heaped onto her shoulders. Because she pressed charges against him for what he did to her. Because he went to prison and lost his license to practice medicine. Because he was desperate, and she could no longer deal with the mood swings and the drama…she had only wanted out of the marriage.

What kind of person did that make her?

The single bite of bread, ham and cheese she had swallowed sat like a rock in her stomach.

"Unfortunately he was dead when the firemen arrived on the scene."

The words pummeled her like stones. She really had left the poor man to die.

"You did not put him in the situation he found himself in, Doc. The man you pulled that bullet out of was Brent Underwood. According to what Bella could find on him, he was one of Anastasia's long-time accountants. Rumor on the street is that he was skimming the books. That doesn't make what happened to him right, but it damned sure tells you he chose his own path."

She forced down another bite. Told herself he was right. This was not her fault any more than William's death was. "So what do we do now?"

"We wait and we rest while we can."

"What if he calls again?" This time when the bite lodged in her throat, she forced it down with a long swig of water.

"We'll deal with that issue when the time comes."

She stared at her plate. Pushed it away. "You make it sound so easy."

"This ain't my first rodeo, Doc." He stacked her plate on top of his. "Most of the cases I investigate involve people who do very bad things. The best I can hope for is to protect the innocent and to help make sure the bad guys don't get away with it."

She couldn't think about this anymore. It was time

for a change of subject. "Do you get back to see your family often?"

He glanced at her as he cleaned up the remains of their dinner. If he was surprised by the abrupt change of topics, he showed no indication. "Every Christmas and every Father's Day."

Father's Day was barely two weeks ago, so he must have just seen him. "So you said your father's still involved with running the ranch despite being retired?" she asked.

He nodded, tucked the plates into the dishwasher. "More than my older brother would prefer, I think."

"What about your mother?" She leaned against the counter, forced her mind away from that warehouse and the man who had died there.

Her bodyguard dried his hands and tossed the towel aside. "She was injured in a horseback riding accident when I was twelve. She died a few hours later. She was a damned good rider, but, as I've gotten older, I've realized that even the best swimmer can drown. Just one of those freak accidents you hope will never happen. But it happened to her."

"That must have been very difficult." She couldn't imagine being twelve and losing her mother. It was bad enough at thirty.

"What about you?"

She looked up at him. "My brother and I grew up in southern Illinois. My mother was a substitute teacher. Dad managed a supermarket. It was a small town so everyone knew everyone else. My parents were determined that both their children would be doctors. I suppose like most, they wanted better for us than they had."

"Your brother's a doctor, too."

"He is. Steven's three years younger than me and still finding himself." She laughed, picturing her brother, the free spirit who felt completely comfortable grabbing his passport and taking off at the drop of a hat. "He spends all his free time traveling, but his travels usually involve volunteering in support of those in areas where there isn't adequate medical care available."

"You lost both your parents." He walked to the coffee maker and started a fresh pot.

"A few years ago. Mother died of cancer, and Dad had a heart attack a couple of years later. It was a tough time." She'd longed for the comfort of simply talking with them when her marriage disintegrated. She hadn't shared the dirty details with her brother until after William was in prison. Her little brother might be younger than her, but he was very protective. She only wished she could see him more often. The once-a-year thing was not nearly enough.

"Sit," he suggested. "I'll serve the coffee. Cream, no sugar, right?"

"Right." She weaved her way around the island and climbed onto one of the stools. "Is this what you do most of the time? I mean, are your cases typically like this one?"

"Sometimes providing protection is involved, sometimes not. Depends on the situation."

The bold smell of fresh-brewed dark roast coffee filled the air.

"Are your clients usually female?" She clasped her hands atop the granite counter and studied her bodyguard. She wondered how many of his clients wanted more than just his protection.

What in the world? She shook herself. Her brain was obviously muddled.

"Two out of three, maybe." He poured the coffee, added cream to hers and then walked toward her with a mug in each hand. "Victoria assigns the best man or woman for the case. Gender has little to do with her decisions."

"Thank you." Marissa wrapped her hands around the warm mug. "I imagine you have plenty of damsels in distress hoping for more than your protection."

The silence that followed exploded in her ears. Had she really asked that question out loud? To think it was bad enough. Oh…dear…God. She really, really needed to go into that room upstairs and close herself inside. What he must think of her!

He finally laughed, a sort of choked sound. "I have to say I haven't encountered that situation yet."

What did the mere thought say about her? The answer echoed in more of that embarrassing silence.

"I think maybe television and the movies glamorize the kind of work I do a little too much. I can see how you might think these situations could easily drift off into a romantic interlude."

Now she was really embarrassed. She tried to laugh, but it came out more like a squeak. "I guess I read too many romance novels growing up. My mother was a big romantic. She had a library of hundreds of books. They all had a couple themes in common—boy rescues girl, girl falls in love with boy."

This time his chuckle was the real thing, the sound pleasant. She liked it. "My mom had one of those, too," he offered. "She and my sister always had a book on their bedside tables."

"How old is your sister?"

"A couple of years older than me. She's a veterinarian. Takes care of the horses and the cattle. You two would get along well. The only difference is her patients generally have four legs."

Marissa was the one laughing this time. It felt good, made her relax marginally.

Traynor told her which of his siblings were married and who wasn't, who had children and who wanted more. He loved his nieces and nephews. Loved his family. The pride in his eyes and in his voice made her smile. She liked listening to his voice. His laughter made her feel normal again. How long had it been since she'd had a conversation like this with anyone besides her colleagues at work? She couldn't even remember.

"I have to say, Mr. Traynor, listening to you talk about your family, you almost sound homesick."

He held her gaze for a long moment. "Sometimes. But my work here makes me happy. I don't see myself going back." He reached for his coffee. "By the way, you have to stop calling me that. Mr. Traynor is my father. Call me Lacon."

"All right, Lacon. Then you should call me Marissa or Issy. That's what my friends call me." She made a face. "Except Eva. She insists on calling me Dr. Frasier whenever we're wearing scrubs and at work. Any other time she calls me Issy, too."

"Issy it is, then."

Her cell vibrated against the granite and she jumped. Blocked Call. Her blood ran cold. "It's him."

"Stay calm," Lacon warned. "Don't let him hear your fear. When you answer, put it on speaker."

She accepted the call and tapped the speaker icon. "Marissa Frasier."

"I wanted to thank you, Doctor."

It was him.

"No need to thank me. I didn't do it for you," she replied, barely keeping a snarl out of her tone. "I did it for the man who'd been shot."

"Be that as it may, I appreciate your work. I was able to extract the information I needed, and I couldn't have done it without your help."

And then his thugs had killed him.

"You son of a bitch!"

Lacon held up his hands and gave her the signal to bring it down.

She tried, she really did, but she was so angry. "I hope you die screaming."

Laughter echoed from the damned phone. It took every ounce of control Marissa possessed not to fling it across the room.

"I would have been disappointed if you hadn't been angry, Dr. Frasier. In fact, I have to give you credit. Having your friend call in the fire department was ingenious. I'm genuinely grateful my men were able to get what I needed before the men in the turn-out gear arrived. You see, if my people had failed and been forced to abandon this traitor, I would have been most unhappy. No one likes it when I'm unhappy, Marissa. May I call you Marissa?"

Lacon silently cautioned her again.

"If this arrangement is going to be so informal, then I'll need to know your name, as well."

A soft laugh whispered in the air. "Vito. You can call me Vito, which is far better than 'son of a bitch.'"

She would not apologize.

Lacon made a hand signal for money. At first she was confused, then she understood.

"If you think I'm going to continue this arrangement out of the goodness of my heart, you're mistaken, Vito. I expect far more than whatever you were paying William."

Another laugh, this one not so soft. "You have one more test before we talk about money. There is one matter, however, we should discuss. Your bodyguard. He cramps my style. Get rid of him."

Fear bloomed in her chest. Lacon shook his head.

She swallowed back the fear. "Except," she countered, sounding almost casual, "now I have you threatening my safety, so no deal."

The silence dragged on long enough to make her sweat.

"I like you, Dr. Marissa Frasier, so I will grant you this one demand. But make no mistake, if you or your bodyguard screw with me, you will both die—screaming, as you say."

The call ended.

Marissa grabbed the countertop to brace herself.

Lacon gave her arm a squeeze. "Really good job, Issy."

She turned to him. "I don't know if I can do what he wants…" She shook her head. "God only knows what the next scene he sends me to will look like." Her body shook with the fear she wanted to keep at bay.

Lacon pulled her to him, gave her a big hug. "You're strong, Issy. You can do this. If you help the police take him down, think how many lives you'll be saving."

She pressed her face against his chest and closed her eyes. "I keep telling myself that's the upside of this situation."

"But any time you want out, say the word and I'll make it happen." He drew her away from him to look into her eyes. "My job is to keep you safe. That's all that matters to me."

She hugged him this time.

Maybe, just maybe, with the help of this man, she could get through this.

Vito Anastasia was going down, by God.

Chapter Six

Saturday, June 30, 7:45 a.m.

Marissa slowed the speed of the treadmill for her final mile. Her heart pounded and sweat clung to her skin. It felt good. She'd missed the stress release that went with a long, hard workout. The entire week had been so busy, she'd fallen behind on her usual workout routine.

The first thing that entered her mind when she woke this morning was the jarring and painful memory that William was dead. In a few days, his family would be claiming his body, there would be a funeral and then he would be laid to rest.

Would she be able to attend his funeral? Should she? They had been in love once. Five years as husband and wife was significant. In truth, she had worked hard to evict any good memories along with the bad ones over the past two years. After what he'd done to her toward the end, who could blame her?

Slowing to a fast walk, she pushed the questions aside. The second thought to pop into her head before she threw back the sheets and climbed out of bed was about Vito Anastasia. He had to be stopped. But the police were right; that wouldn't happen until they had a significant body of evidence to make it happen. They needed a way in, a way to get close to him. All she had to do was play along until *she* could make that happen. For whatever reason, fate had dropped that terrifying potential into her lap.

How could she ignore the possibility of taking one more ruthless murderer off the streets?

The treadmill stopped and she swabbed her face with the towel hanging around her neck. The thought of dealing with another injured person Anastasia might murder made her shudder. But he would never stop unless someone stopped him.

She could be that someone. All she needed was the right kind of backup.

Traynor—Lacon—was her protector. He'd made it clear that his top priority was to protect her. She was very grateful to have the Colby Agency backing her up. But would he be willing to cross certain lines and boundaries for her? She wasn't a cop. She wasn't tied to the same rules. There were things she could say and steps she could take where Anastasia was concerned that the police could not.

She had heard the interest in Anastasia's voice. For some reason, he was intrigued by her. Or maybe that part had been her imagination, though she didn't think so. He'd also acquiesced to her demand to keep Lacon around. Perhaps she was reading too much into the conversation, but she had nothing to lose by exploring the potential.

Except the same thing William had lost—her life.

You have to be smarter, Issy. William was desperate. Desperation breeds mistakes. If she could keep her wits about her, she could do this. For William and all the other victims Anastasia had taken and would take in the future.

She could help stop him. *Maybe.*

After she'd showered and dressed in a pair of the jeans and a T-shirt she'd packed, she went in search of Lacon. She found him in the kitchen pouring orange juice. Bacon, eggs and toast waited on the stove.

"Good morning." He set the bottle of juice aside. "You feel like breakfast?"

Today she was starving. "I do. Thanks."

He passed her a plate and they met in front of the stove. He wore jeans and a button-down cotton shirt—this one in white—much like yesterday. And, of course, the cowboy boots. Another of those casual suit jackets hung on the back of one of the stools facing the large island. Today's jacket was navy. Somehow the outfit was perfect for the man. She couldn't imagine him in a dress suit.

"I wasn't sure how you liked your eggs, so I figured scrambled was the way to go."

"This is exactly how I like my eggs."

His smile was contagious. "Good."

Marissa settled onto a stool and dug in. The eggs were soft, the bacon crispy and the toast lightly buttered. Certainly not her usual fare of yogurt and granola, but so scrumptious. Maybe it all tasted so good because she'd hardly eaten in the past forty-eight hours. The ER had been so busy Thursday night, she'd barely had time to grab a bag of veggie chips.

Or maybe it was just because she was alive and not dead.

When she'd slowed down, she asked, "Any news on the drug tests?"

"Ian Michaels called first thing this morning. You tested positive for Rohypnol. We haven't heard from PD's lab yet, but I'm sure they'll find it in the bottle of wine you drank from that night, and something similar in Bauer's tox screen, as well."

"Wow." She placed her fork next to her plate as the news traveled through her.

The confirmation that one of Anastasia's men came into her home and laced her bottle of wine with a date rape drug made her furious. As a teenager and a college student, she had been extra careful about having so much as a soda in public places where her drink might be left unattended even for a second. The fact that this drink—this drug—had been administered in her own home, in a bottle of her wine, made her feel ill.

The queasy feeling abruptly morphed into outrage. "I will not allow him to get away with this. If there is any way I can help stop him, I'm up for it."

"We're doing all we can toward that end, as well," Lacon promised.

She wanted to tell him, to blurt out the decision she'd made this morning, but that wouldn't be the smart move. He would see the emotion behind the announcement. When the time was right, her words had to be calm and logical.

"I know you are." She picked up her plate and fork. "Thanks for the breakfast. I didn't know chef was a part of your repertoire of skills."

He chuckled as he followed her to the sink. "Chef, personal shopper, chauffeur—it all goes with the territory."

Putting her cleaned plate into the dishwasher, she asked, "Do you ever make operational decisions without consulting the boss?"

"There are times when—" he placed his plate behind hers "—split-second decisions have to be made. At the Colby Agency, we receive extensive training and daily briefings. Victoria trusts her investigators to make the right decisions."

Marissa doubted very seriously if the operational decision she wanted him to make fell within the agency's approved guidelines. "Victoria is right to trust you." She peered up at her bodyguard and again acknowledged the warmth in his eyes. "You were spot-on with every move last night. If I had any doubts about any aspect of moving forward, they disappeared when you made that call to summon the fire department to help that man."

"Unfortunately it didn't help."

"True." She nodded. "But you tried, and that effort helped me tremendously."

He held her gaze, searching her eyes. Was he looking for the motive behind her words? Did he sense that she was up to something? He was, after all, a top-notch investigator trained to spot potential issues.

Her cell vibrated and she jumped. She snatched it from her hip pocket, her pulse racing as she considered the possibility that it could be Anastasia again.

Please don't let it be him.

The number was the staff line at the Edge.

"Marissa Frasier."

Lacon watched her expectantly. She mouthed the word *work*. He nodded.

"Dr. Frasier, this is Patsy. I realize this is your weekend off, but Jeremiah Owens's mother is here and she says it's imperative that she speak with you in person." The rustle of sounds on the other end indicated Patsy had moved to a different location. "She seems pretty upset. What would you like me to do?"

Fear thumped in Marissa's veins. "Tell her it'll take me about forty-five minutes to get there, but I'll leave right now and head that way."

"I'll tell her. Thanks, Dr. Frasier."

Marissa slid her phone back into her pocket. “It’s the Owens boy’s mother. She wants to speak with me in person.”

Lacon reached for the keys on the counter. “We should see what she has to say.”

If Anastasia had harmed that child in any way…

Well, Marissa would make him pay. Somehow.

The Edge, 10:00 a.m.

MARISSA HAD WORKED herself up by the time they reached the Edge. She fluctuated between utter outrage and sheer terror. She should have called Jeremiah’s mother to check on him. She could have done so without giving away why she was calling. If something had happened to the boy, it would be her fault.

She hurried to the desk and waited for Patsy to finish registering a new arrival. As soon as the elderly man had shuffled away, the registration specialist said, “I put her in the small conference room.”

Marissa thanked Patsy and headed for the double doors that separated the large lobby that served as a waiting room and the emergency department. Lacon was right behind her. She waved to Nurse Kim Levy and hurried past the nurses’ station to the small conference room.

Mrs. Owens sat alone, her hands wringing together atop the small round conference table. Her worried face lit up as Marissa walked in. "I'm so sorry to bother you on your day off."

Marissa slid into a chair next to her. She patted the woman's clasped hands. "No problem. Is Jeremiah okay?"

She nodded. "He's doing fine. But I wanted to ask you about those men."

The bottom dropped out of Marissa's stomach. "What men?"

"Two men have been watching my house. They were there all day yesterday, and they're back today. I finally worked up my nerve this morning and walked out to the car. I asked the driver if there was a problem, and he said no. He said they were just keeping an eye on things and that they're friends of yours. I'm not trying to be mean, but they make me very nervous."

Fury roared through Marissa's blood. "I will take care of this, Mrs. Owens. There's been a miscommunication. Those men aren't supposed to be there. You go home and don't worry about this anymore."

She nodded, relief washing over her face. "I figured there was a mix-up of some sort." Her face pinched with worry once more. "I hope whoever those men are supposed to be looking after is okay."

"They're fine. Just fine."

Marissa, with Lacon right next to her, walked her back to the lobby. "Thank you for coming by. I really am sorry for the confusion."

When Owens was halfway across the lobby, Marissa yanked her phone from her pocket once more. She sent a text to the contact who had sent her Anastasia's instructions last night. The message was brief and straight to the point.

Tell Anastasia to call me. Now.

Surprise sent Lacon's eyebrows shooting up. "That should get his attention."

Marissa stormed back to the conference room to wait on a response. She did not want to be closed up in a car if she was able to speak with him. Lacon closed the door behind her and took a seat. She couldn't sit. She paced the small room, anger building with every step she took.

"You might want to take a breath," he suggested.

She stalled and flashed him a fake smile. "I am breathing."

He held up his hands. "Okay."

As angry as she was, she stalled and did as he said. She inhaled long and deep, let it out slowly. A couple more times, and her heart rate had calmed somewhat. Her phone vibrated and she snatched it from her pocket.

Blocked Call.

"I think it's him." She accepted the call. "Marissa Frasier."

"Dr. Frasier." He sighed. "You are determined to test my patience."

"Call your dogs off the Owens home. I did what you asked—now I want you to leave them alone."

Lacon sat back in his chair, his arms crossed over his chest. She couldn't decide if that amused smile he wore was about pity or pride.

Silence, thick and suffocating, reverberated across the line.

"Your friend the bodyguard should explain the hierarchy in this relationship, Dr. Frasier." Anastasia's voice was cold, hard. "He's employed by the Colby Agency. I'm certain he's well aware of how things work."

"If you don't live up to your side of the bargain," Marissa warned as if he hadn't said a word, "then there is no relationship. Leave the Owens family alone."

More of that tense silence filled the air. Her heart thumped harder and harder with each second that elapsed.

"Done."

The call ended. Marissa stared at the screen. Could it really have been so easy?

Lacon stood. "You okay?"

She shrugged. "I honestly don't know."

He chuckled. "I have to tell you, Issy, I'm torn between being damned impressed and freaking terrified."

A laugh burst from her, but before she could say she felt basically the same way, the door opened and

Kim poked her head into the room. "A balcony collapsed while a bridal party was taking photos on it. We've got fourteen injured five minutes out. Dr. Reagan wondered if you might be able to help out for a couple of hours."

"Glad to." She glanced at Lacon.

"Don't worry about me. Do what you've got to do. I have calls to make."

Marissa wasn't exactly dressed for work, but that hardly mattered. She washed up, donned a white coat and was ready by the time the lead ambulance rolled in.

The first gurney to come through the doors was the bride. Marissa moved toward trauma room one with the paramedics.

"Caroline Boehner, twenty-seven, BP one fifty over ninety, pulse a hundred ten. Complaining of pain in the right leg."

"Thank you." Marissa put a hand on the young woman's arm. "Don't worry, Caroline, we're going to get you taken care of. You'll be ready for that walk down the aisle in no time."

The younger woman's mascara had made black streaks down her cheeks. The updo her blond hair had been arranged into had come undone. Beyond the tangled mass of hair, her veil appeared to be intact. The beaded bodice of her gown had managed to avoid damage, but the lower portion of the mermaid-style lace-and-tulle train had not fared so well. Whatever shoes she'd been wearing were long gone.

"Are my parents okay?" A sob tore from her throat. "I'm so worried about them. We were doing the photos—you know, the ones you do before the wedding." More tears flowed down her face. "My whole family was on that balcony."

Marissa gave her arm a squeeze and turned to the paramedic. "We'll get you an update on everyone as soon as we can. For now, let's get you taken care of."

After a quick examination, Marissa sent the bride off to Imaging. The six bridesmaids and the flower girl were all treated and released with nothing more than scrapes and bruises. The bride's two brothers and one sister, who was the maid of honor, were shaken and bruised but had no serious injuries. The mother suffered a fracture of the left scapular body.

By far the worst injury was the father's, a hip fracture that would require surgery. The sixty-year-old man was in excellent physical condition, so there was every reason to be optimistic about a speedy recovery. The bride suffered a stable fracture in the tibial shaft. Surprisingly, there wasn't one concussion among the whole lot.

They were a very lucky group.

The groom and the rest of the wedding party arrived and filled the lobby. Anyone else coming in would think a wedding was imminent right there in front of the registration desk. Thankfully, the news

Marissa had to pass along was all reasonably good, considering the fall the bride's party had taken.

When the last patient was out the door and the ER was quiet again, Kim watched as Marissa peeled off her gloves and left the white coat in the laundry hamper.

Marissa shot her a look. "What?"

"So, tall, blond and handsome is your bodyguard?"

Marissa laughed. She couldn't help herself. "He is."

"Wow. I mean, I know you're still reeling from what happened to Dr. Bauer, but the two of you were divorced for a really long time before…he died. And you've hardly dated since. Seriously, you should enjoy some of that."

"Some of that?" Marissa dried her hands, thankful they were in the locker room. "What on earth are you suggesting?"

Kim pushed away from the door frame. "I'm suggesting, Doctor, that you relax and let go. You're always so busy giving that you never take anything for yourself. Take something!" She threw her hands in the air for emphasis. "Something gorgeous and hot and better than six feet tall."

Rather than scold her friend as she normally would have, Marissa nodded slowly. "I'll take it under advisement."

Kim rolled her eyes. "You are so predictable."

Ah, if she only knew. "The one thing I am not these days, Kim, is predictable."

"Where your love life is concerned you are." Kim sent her a look daring her to counter that statement.

Love life. Marissa didn't have a love life. The most recent three men in her life were her deceased ex-husband, a mob boss and a bodyguard. Even if she were in the market, it was hard to make anything romantic out of the combination.

"I saw him watching you," Kim argued. "He thinks you're hot."

Marissa laughed out loud. "Okay, I think that's my cue to get out of here."

"Just sayin'."

"As you said from the outset, this is not exactly the right time for romance," Marissa pointed out.

Kim gave her a skeptical look. "Who said anything about romance? I'm talking about sex. Hot, down-and-dirty, mind-blowing sex."

Before Marissa could summon a proper response, her friend hustled off to check on her patients. Marissa sighed and went in search of Lacon. He was waiting for her at the nurses' station. Every female on duty smiled at him and called goodbye.

The man was undeniably handsome, cowboy boots and all.

Marissa shook her head at the foolish notion. She had a mob boss to take down. This was no time for sex, not even the hot, down-and-dirty, mind-blowing kind.

Colby Safe House, 9:30 p.m.

MARISSA STARED AT the glass of wine in her hand. If she had been impressed with Lacon Traynor's breakfast-making skills, she was truly fascinated by his prowess at the grill. Steaks and potatoes and a nice, leafy green salad. When she'd asked him how he'd acquired such a command of the culinary arts, he'd simply replied that being single and closer to forty than thirty, it was either learn to cook or starve.

When he'd first offered the wine, she'd passed, but the more he'd made her laugh during dinner, the more she'd relaxed, and a couple of glasses of wine began to sound far more appealing. He'd stopped at one, and she'd felt a little guilty when she moved on to number two. But not that guilty. She sipped her wine. Rich, red and bold flavored. She needed the relief—that was a certainty.

"According to Anastasia," she said, abruptly recalling the conversation, "you should be able to tell me all about him and how the hierarchy of my new relationship with him works."

Her bodyguard considered the statement from his relaxed position on the sofa. She'd curled up in one of the massive upholstered chairs for the best view of the water. Rather than answer her right away, he pulled off his right boot, then he moved on to the left. He set them side by side on the floor.

Marissa frowned. "Do you always wear boots?"

"Most of the time." He leaned back and propped his sock-clad feet on the large leather ottoman. "I have running shoes for working out. And the boots." His shoulders went up and then down in an easy shrug. "That's about it."

To avoid staring at his long lean body like a smitten schoolgirl, she said, "Tell me what makes Anastasia so special." She wanted to make the bastard feel the pain he inflicted upon his victims. Despite the wine, anger simmered inside her.

"He's young to be sitting at the top. Forty-two. He's doing all in his power to resurrect the 'family,' as he calls it. He's smarter than the average criminal. Ruthless. Single. No children. So he has basically nothing to lose. It's hard to best a man who doesn't have an Achilles' heel."

"Except he wants to win," Marissa decided. "Power is his weakness."

"You're saying that he's so fixated on getting what he wants that he might not see what's right in front of him?"

"Exactly. Psych 101." She downed the last of the wine and set her glass aside. "Is he unmarried and childless because he's so focused that he ignores his own needs? If so, that makes him a ticking time bomb. Eventually, that kind of focus comes back to haunt you. You can't ignore what the mind and body require forever."

Lacon assessed her for an endless moment. “Sounds like words spoken from experience.”

She assessed him right back. “Experience we have in common.”

A grin hitched up one side of his mouth. “Touché.”

They lapsed into silence for long enough to make her feel restless. She pushed out of her chair and went to the wall of windows. The sun had set, leaving the moon to reflect its golden glow on the water. Way out here, away from the city, the world felt so peaceful, so quiet. So innocent.

“Why did you become a doctor?” He moved up beside her, his gaze settling on the dark water.

“Because I wanted to help people.” She crossed her arms and leaned against the window frame. “And it was all my mom and dad ever talked about.”

“Have you ever regretted your decision to go into medicine?”

“Never.” A smile tugged at her lips. “I spend a lot of time working with kids. I donate every other weekend to the Chicago Children’s Center. I love seeing them smile when they’re happy. It makes my heart glad to see the relief on their parents’ faces when I tell them everything will be fine.”

“What about when you can’t tell them everything will be fine?”

He was watching her closely now, as if the answer was somehow incredibly important to him.

"It's the most painful thing I've ever felt. In that moment, I would give anything to have a different answer."

"Is that why you didn't have children of your own?"

She met his analyzing gaze. "No. William didn't want children right away. Then it was always later, later. When everything fell apart, it no longer mattered. I guess I assumed I'd one day meet someone new and things would be different, but that window is closing all too quickly."

"You deserve things to be different," he said softly. "And that window is far from closed."

"What about you?" She lifted her chin and made the same deduction about him. "Don't you deserve for things to be different in your personal life? A wife, kids, maybe?"

"What makes you think I want anything different from what I have right now?"

Maybe he didn't. Maybe she had misjudged him. "I don't know. You just seem a little lonely when it's quiet like this and no one needs rescuing."

He reached out, tugged at a wisp of her curly hair. "How could I be lonely with you standing right there?"

His fingertips traced her cheek, trailed down her throat, moved around her neck and pulled her close. Her breath caught, but she didn't resist. Deep down she'd wanted to know what he tasted like from the moment they met.

His lips closed over hers, and the taste of wine and man had her melting against him.

He drew away all too soon. “As much as I would like to, it’s probably best that we don’t cross that line tonight, Issy.”

She curled her fingers in his shirtfront and held him close when he would have moved away. “We’re both adults. We can do whatever we like.” Her voice was thick with the desire sizzling in her veins.

“You think about that, and if you don’t change your mind, we’ll revisit the subject tomorrow or the next day.”

She released him and he walked away. She watched him go before turning her attention back to the moon and those glittering stars that she never saw in the city.

The truth was, she’d already made up her mind. Going after Vito Anastasia was incredibly dangerous. She could end up dead just like William.

Maybe it was the wine, but at the moment, she could not imagine dying without knowing Lacon Traynor intimately first.

Chapter Seven

Sunday, July 1, 5:30 a.m.

Marissa lay in the darkness. She didn't want to get up. What she wanted was to lie right here and keep replaying that brief but incredibly sexy kiss over and over. Almost two years, that was how long it had been since she'd been kissed—really kissed—even just briefly. Sure, she'd had the peck on the cheek from friends after an evening out or in thanks for the perfect birthday present. But a real kiss, cloaked in desire that burned all the way through her, had not landed on her lips or anywhere else on her body in so very long.

Of all the times for her libido to suddenly turn itself back on. She closed her eyes and replayed one more time the tender way his lips—lips that had looked so firm and yet felt so soft—had molded to hers. The sweet, hot taste of his mouth and, mercy, the feel of his fingers tracing her skin. She shivered, feeling warm and needy.

In medical school and then in her residency, she'd done psych rotations and she'd completed the necessary coursework, but it didn't take a psychiatrist to comprehend the problem here. The murder of her ex-husband and the fear and chaos of being drawn into the dangerous world he'd crashed into since his release from jail had her survival instinct in overdrive.

Her reaction was completely natural. Faced with the possibility of death, the instinctive response was a relentless urge to procreate—to celebrate the mating of the human body. No great mystery. The problem was her instincts didn't quite understand that she was like a starving person suddenly faced with a mouthwatering buffet. She wanted desperately to assuage the emptiness and insecurity smothering her with what he had to offer well beyond his ability to keep her safe.

Not a smart move, Issy.

She climbed out of bed and dragged on a pair of jeans and another T-shirt. The outfit was the last of the casual wear she'd brought with her. She'd have to try out the laundry room at some point today or get permission to stop by her house for fresh clothes. Considering her name and face had already shown up in the news related to William's murder, she had no desire to go shopping. Stuffing her feet into her sneakers without bothering to untie them, she reached for her phone, tucked it into her back pocket and then thumbed the backs of the shoes over her heels.

Lacon was probably already downstairs prowling around in the kitchen. If not, she didn't mind taking her turn to prepare breakfast. She was far from a great cook, but she made a mean egg sandwich. She'd hit the bottom step of the grand staircase when she smelled the pancakes. Her stomach rumbled. She could get used to this.

Lacon stood at the stove, a dishtowel slung over his shoulder. She paused at the door and watched as he flipped pancakes onto a plate. Like her, he wore jeans again today, paired with a khaki-colored shirt this time and the boots, of course. The usual jacket, this one black, hung on a chair at the table.

She enjoyed watching the sure movements of his hands—broad, long-fingered hands. She'd felt his arms, his chest. There was plenty of hard muscle beneath all that soft cotton. Long muscular legs and a great backside that filled out the jeans he wore. Kim, damn her, had sparked her imagination, and now it was running away with her. She sighed.

The object of her naughty musings glanced over his shoulder as if he'd sensed her presence or heard that sigh of defeat. "Morning."

"Morning." She pushed away from the door and went to the fridge. "Orange juice?"

"Yes, ma'am. Nothing goes with pancakes like orange juice."

"Except—" she reached for two glasses "—sausage and syrup."

"That part goes without saying. Pancakes aren't pancakes without syrup and sausage. It's a rule."

She laughed as she poured the juice. A tiny part of her wanted to feel ashamed that she could laugh and feel desire so soon after William's death, but that wasn't fair. Their relationship had been over for two years. Though she certainly still had feelings for him, those feelings were more about basic human compassion, the loss of an old friend…of the man who had once been the center of her universe. In reality, she had grieved the loss of their love and the intimate part of their relationship years ago. She refused to continue blaming herself for William's problems or for what she might have done differently.

It was well past time she moved on. As soon as she helped put Vito Anastasia where he belonged.

One some level she recognized that she should be afraid, terrified even. But the man flipping those pancakes made her stronger, braver, not to mention desperate for another of his kisses.

"Anything new this morning?"

It was likely too early, but it never hurt to ask. One of his colleagues from the Colby Agency may have called him already or sent him an update by email or text. She doubted their investigations operated on a nine-to-five schedule.

"Nothing new yet." He carried the two plates loaded with pancakes and sausage links to the table. "Grab the syrup."

She set the glasses on the table and returned to the counter for the syrup. Old-fashioned maple, her favorite. "Will the police keep me updated on their investigation into William's murder?" She had no idea how this worked. She'd never personally known anyone who was murdered.

"The two detectives will contact you as necessary. They don't like to give up too much information during the course of an investigation, so don't expect a lot of interaction—unless they need information they believe you have."

Since she'd told them everything she knew, she didn't expect to hear from them anytime soon unless it was to do the formal statement. They ate for a while without saying more. There really wasn't a lot more to say. It felt as if they were in a time warp, and everything relevant to the out-of-control situation had suddenly stopped.

Her cell vibrated. She stilled. Lowered her fork to her plate and reached into her hip pocket. *Please don't let it be him.*

Blocked Call.

Dread swelled in her belly, pushing away her appetite and making her heart thump harder. "It's him."

Lacon gave her a nod. "Answer it."

God, she did not want to. What if he demanded that she go to another scene like the one she'd gone to yesterday?

She accepted the call and immediately set the phone to speaker. "Marissa Frasier."

"I need you, Dr. Frasier."

His voice, cold, calculating, twisted her insides. Without giving her time to question his demand, he stated the address and severed the connection.

She stared at the phone for a moment, her stomach churning, threatening to rebel against the few bites of breakfast she'd taken.

"We'll need forty minutes to get there," Lacon said.

Nodding slowly, she tucked her phone away. "Do we tell anyone?"

He stood. "Never make a move in an op like this without keeping your backup informed. That mistake is the fastest way I know to get yourself dead."

Nothing like another dash of reality to undermine her bravado.

FIVE MINUTES LATER they were en route. Lacon gave Ian Michaels a heads-up. Michaels would coordinate with their contact at Chicago PD. Issy spent the better portion of the drive lost in thought, or maybe she was mentally preparing herself for what she might have to do.

Don't let it be like last time. He didn't want her to have to go through that again.

Lacon liked this plan less and less. He didn't see an end to Anastasia's use of her as a pawn. The bastard was far too careful to get himself caught in a trap so easily foreseeable. Bottom line, something had to give soon. Every event like the one they were about to walk into endangered her life.

While every night they spent together tested his ability to maintain control.

That kiss. That damned foolish idea that he could scare her off by making a move. Damn it. All he'd accomplished was to fan the flames already blazing inside him. He wanted to know her...every inch of her.

Backing away from that perilous cliff, he focused on the here and now. Their destination was a small older convenience store located at the corner of Hirsch and Kildare. He parked near the front entrance. There were no other cars near the store. They were probably parked in the back.

From the outside, the store looked closed. He emerged from the car, scanned the area and moved around to the passenger side. Issy was already climbing out. As they approached the front entrance, the single glass door with its steel bars opened. Like the thugs from yesterday, the man wore a mask. Fury had Lacon gritting his teeth. He hoped like hell these bastards got what they deserved.

Soon.

The goon took Lacon's weapon, locked the door behind them and then led the way to the storage area at the back of the building where stock was kept. Two men lay on the vinyl-tiled floor. Both were dressed in black, sans the masks. Their battered faces appeared to be the least of their worries. Blood had soaked their shirts and leaked onto the floor. The most telling aspect of the situation was that neither of the two masked thugs was aiming their weapons at them. The injured were part of their team. One of them, the one farthest from where they stood, kept trying to raise himself up onto his elbows.

"It's about damned time," the injured guy doing the moving growled. "What the hell took you so long?"

"What happened?" Issy moved toward the first of the two victims and lowered to her knees. She didn't bother responding to the other guy.

"A disagreement over a debt," the second of the masked men said.

Lacon recognized the voice. Same top thug as before. *Bastard.*

He surveyed the space. This time a bag of medical supplies sat on the floor next to where the men lay. Issy tugged on a pair of gloves then passed a second pair to Lacon. "I may need your help."

"You got it." He pulled on the gloves and crouched down beside her.

"Have they been given anything for pain?"

Since the two weren't howling in agony, Lacon was reasonably sure they'd been given something to take the edge off.

Top Thug confirmed it. Issy shot him a disgusted look and then prepared to open the shirt of the first victim. From the slit in the fabric, it was evident he'd done a little dance with a knife. When the shirt-front was pulled apart, a nasty laceration about eight inches wide made a bloody smile across his abdomen. There was a lot of blood, and the guy grumbled about needing something more for the pain.

"I need to explore this wound to ensure the penetration didn't reach into the abdominal cavity and nick an organ." She nodded to the other guy. "Have a look at his injuries for me. If there's a BP cuff in the bag, check that for me, as well."

The guy who wanted to sit up spewed a few more curses.

Lacon moved into position next to the grumpy patient. "Be still," he ordered. When the guy had relaxed onto the floor, Lacon ripped open his bloody shirt. Two bullet holes to the torso. There was a lot of blood still oozing from the wounds. "Two entrance wounds just above the naval." He rolled the guy forward just enough to check for any exit wounds, prompting some angry curses. "Got one exit wound to the lower back." He pushed the damaged shirt a little higher up his back. "Don't see a second one. Looks like a .38."

When he allowed the man to settle back against the floor, the thug kept his mouth shut. His face had paled, and he seemed to have lost interest in complaining. "You want me to check his BP?"

"Try to stop the bleeding," Issy ordered. "I'll cover this wound and change patients with you." She nodded toward the grumpy guy who'd decided to keep quiet for now. "I need to have a closer look at him before I finish here."

Lacon applied pressure to the two wounds that were no more than two inches apart. The bleeding eased somewhat, but the glazed look in the guy's eyes told him things were going south. "That's probably a good idea. I don't think he's doing too well."

Dividing his attention between Issy and the two thugs hovering over them, he noticed one of the bastards appeared to be videotaping the whole thing like an episode of some reality show. Probably an order from Anastasia. His increasing interest in Issy was more than a little troubling.

Issy quickly peeled off the bloody gloves and stretched on a new pair. She hurried around to get into position next to Lacon. "Keep an eye on the other guy. I'll want that bag closer so I can grab what I need from here."

Lacon scooted the bag next to her. When he'd

changed his gloves and covertly taken what he needed from his pocket, he knelt down next to the guy with the laceration to the gut. He made a show of checking his injury, ensuring that the fingers of his right hand dipped into the man's trouser pocket.

"She gonna finish patching me up?" he asked.

Lacon gave him a nod. "As soon as she takes care of your friend."

Issy tore a scalpel from its packaging and used it to make an incision between the wounds to facilitate getting a closer look inside his gut. She shook her head. "I need more light."

"There's one of those headlights in the bag," Top Thug told her.

Lacon reached across the two injured men and dug around until he located the headlight. He turned on the spotlight and held it in place. Judging by Issy's face and her voice when she'd asked for the light, the situation was deteriorating quickly.

She mumbled a *thanks* as she carefully examined the area she'd opened. Lacon monitored the guys with the guns. Blood abruptly oozed far faster from the wound she was probing. She swore and worked to find the source. The seconds ticked off, and her attempts were futile. The blood just kept coming. The patient was obviously going into shock from the blood loss. He'd gone still as stone and barely blinked.

"We need to get this man to the ER!" she shouted

at the two thugs. "I can't do what needs to be done for him here."

"No hospital," Top Thug tossed back. "It's your job to fix him. Now. Here."

Tension rifled through Lacon. She was losing this battle. Blood continued to pour out of the man now.

She looked up at Lacon. "Call 911 or we're going to lose him."

He reached for his phone just as a muzzle bored into the back of his skull. "Move and I will blow your head off."

Issy swore again as she fought to get the bleeding under control. "He's dying," she snapped. "I cannot make the necessary repairs using what you've given me to work with!"

"Can I help?" Lacon said, the phone in his hand seeming to burn his palm. He should call the guy's bluff. Make the phone call.

"Check his pulse," she ordered. "You may need to start CPR while I..."

Her words trailed off but Lacon didn't hesitate. He pulled the headlight around his head so he could still direct some light toward the injury, tuned out all else and focused on finding that rhythmic beat at the base of the man's throat.

Nothing. "No pulse."

"Begin CPR." Her entire focus was on the wound and stopping the bleeding.

Lacon tossed his phone aside and began the chest

compressions. His instincts said it was too late, but he would do whatever Issy told him to do until she made that call.

Two or three minutes later, she sat back and shook her head. "It's over."

The look of defeat, of desolation on her face tore Lacon apart.

"What about me?" the other guy shouted.

"Move away from the body," Top Thug ordered. "And take care of him." He waved his gun toward the other man.

The thug who had been recording the ordeal tucked his phone away and waited for Lacon and Issy to move away from the dead man.

The defeat gone now, replaced by absolute fury burning from her eyes and hatred etched in her face, Issy stood and peeled off her gloves. Her T-shirt and jeans were a bloody mess. "And what about infections? I can make the necessary repairs to your friend here, but he'll need an antibiotic, and even that might not be enough. Don't you understand this is not a sterile environment?"

"Just do it," Top Thug commanded.

Lacon stared at the man, hoping he saw the intense need to tear him apart in his eyes as he peeled off his gloves. He itched to kick this guy's ass. For Issy's sake, he restrained the urge. This guy wasn't worth risking her life.

With clean gloves, she made quick work of cleaning and closing the laceration to the man's abdomen.

As soon as a dressing was applied, Top Thug ordered, "Get out."

When she'd removed her gloves, Lacon pulled Issy tight to his side as he ushered her toward the front of the store. Just outside the door, Top Thug returned his weapon and slammed the door shut, locking them out. Lacon guided her to the car and settled her into the passenger seat. He fastened her seat belt and hustled around to the driver's side. Rage roared inside him.

There had to be a way to stop this insanity.

For her.

He glanced at Issy repeatedly as he drove. She didn't speak, just stared out the front window, barely so much as blinking.

She couldn't take much more of this.

They'd barely gone a dozen blocks when she spoke. "Stop the car."

He glanced at her. "What's wrong?"

Dumb question. Right now the whole world was wrong. She'd had to watch a man die because she didn't have the necessary tools to save him. Her pleas to call 911 had gone unheeded. The dead man's blood was all over her, the smell thickening inside the car.

"Stop the car," she repeated, her voice so low he could scarcely hear her.

He pulled over at a gas station that had closed

down. Windows and doors were boarded up. Gas pumps were missing.

She flung the door open and hurried to the edge of the parking lot where old broken concrete hit grass, and dropped to her knees.

Lacon got out more slowly, surveying the area for any trouble. When he felt confident they were safe, he lowered to his knees next to her. He held her hair back as she vomited. When the heaving had stopped, she sat for a long moment. He squeezed her shoulder. "You okay?"

She nodded.

He helped her up and they walked back to the car. She said nothing else, and he wished like hell there was more he could say or do.

Her ex-husband had screwed her over, had thrown away his own life and left her to clean up the mess.

Lacon slid back behind the wheel and drove. To his way of thinking, there was only one way to end this—a bullet right between Vito Anastasia's eyes. The sooner the better.

He hoped like hell he was the man who got to pull the trigger for that one.

Maybe that tracking device he'd tucked into the trouser pocket of the guy with the knife wound would provide the first step toward that end.

Chapter Eight

Colby Safe House, 10:08 a.m.

Marissa stood in the middle of the bathroom. She couldn't seem to make herself move. She stared at her hands. Blood still stained the lines and creases, no matter that she'd washed them twice already. That man—in spite of the fact that he had been a criminal and had likely done terrible things—hadn't deserved to die on the floor from injuries that could very likely have been taken care of in the proper medical setting.

How many times had William done this for that son of a bitch Anastasia?

For years she had recognized his lies, knew he kept secrets. Why had she stayed so long after realizing the sort of man he had become?

Her body started to shake. She really had no idea how long she had been standing here in this same spot. Lacon had driven her back to the safe house and ushered her through her room and into this bathroom so she could shower. He'd said he would be back to check on her after his shower.

How long ago had that been?

She told her body to move, to do what needed to be done, but she couldn't seem to make it happen. What she really wanted to do was collapse onto the floor in a pathetic heap and cry until there was no more regret, no more pain and no more fear of what might be coming next. But how would that help anything? If she fell apart, she would be no good to anyone else, let alone herself.

She needed to shower. She stared at the blood soaked into the clothes she wore. It was mostly dry now, though the smell was sickening. But she didn't care how it smelled. Not really. She was too tired to care. What hurt was the reality that all the blood represented a lost life. Part of her just wanted to go to the bed and crawl under the covers.

She stared down at her feet. Somehow she'd managed to toe off her shoes and peel off her socks. She'd left them by the sink downstairs in the laundry room when she'd tried to scrub the blood from her hands—an effort that hadn't worked too well.

Forcing one foot in front of the other, she walked toward the shower. She reached inside and turned on the water. Her fingers found their way to the hem of her T-shirt. All she had to do was pull it up and over her head but somehow she could not. Images of the man who had died this morning flickered in her head. The face of the other man—the one Anastasia's people had murdered after she took care of him—joined the stream of images. She should have done more for both of those men. They were dead, in part, because of her.

She opened the glass door and stepped into the shower. Didn't matter that she still had on her clothes. She no longer cared. She leaned her head against the cool tile wall and allowed the hot water to pound against her back. Her eyes closed and she struggled to hold in the sobs, but they would not be contained.

Wilting helplessly against the wall, she slid down onto her knees. The steam rose, swirling around the sobs echoing from her throat that were tearing at her heart.

The door opened, drawing the heated air out and allowing the cooler air to rush in. She opened her eyes but she didn't move. Didn't care if Anastasia himself was coming for her. She just wanted this nightmare to be over.

Lacon crouched next to her, the water raining down on his blond head, slipping down his muscular shoulders and chest, soaking into the waistband of his jeans. She blinked just to make sure she hadn't imagined him.

"Come here." He helped her up when all she

wanted to do was let the hot water melt her and wash her away. “I’ll take care of you,” he whispered.

His hands found the hem of her T-shirt and pulled it upward. She instinctively raised her arms so he could pull the sticky T-shirt up and over her head. He tossed it onto the built-in bench on the other side of the shower. She closed her eyes and let the hot water patter against her chest. His hands unfastened her jeans. Her eyelids fluttered open, and she watched his long fingers and broad hands work the wet jeans over her hips, down her thighs. She raised one foot and then the other for him to pull the denim free. The stained jeans landed next to the T-shirt.

Then he stood, water rushing over his gorgeous body, soaking into his clean jeans. She realized suddenly that he’d already had his shower. She scrubbed her arm across her face, the hot water mixing with her salty tears. A shudder of defeat quaked through her and she wanted to collapse on the floor once more, but he pulled her into his arms and held her against his strong, warm body.

She cried some more, wishing she could stop, but she couldn’t. He held her, caressed her wet hair and her back. Eventually he drew her away from the comfort of his body and leaned her against the tile wall. It was slick and hot now, no longer cold. He reached for the body wash and filled his palm. Slowly, so very slowly, he smoothed the cherry-blossom-scented soap over her skin. He started with her throat, then traced his hands over her shoulders, down her chest, over the silk encasing her breasts…down her arms.

Her body trembled at his touch. Fire rushed over her skin wherever his hands landed. He clasped his fingers with hers, washing her hands, then traced a trail up her sides. With a gentle prompt, he turned her around and washed her back. Every inch of skin was caressed and massaged thoroughly.

He leaned close, whispered against her temple, "Close your eyes."

Her breath catching at the nearness of his lips, she did as he asked. His every touch, every move was so very gentle. He ushered her under the spray of water and began washing her hair, massaging her scalp until goose bumps spilled over her skin. When he'd rinsed it thoroughly, he started all over again with the conditioner, slowly, methodically working a kind of magic she had never felt before. Her body was on fire, so hot and languid she could barely stand.

Then he dropped to his knees and washed her feet, her ankles, calves and thighs, his touch patient, intent. When she thought he might stop, he added more body wash to his hands and washed her intimately through the strappy bikini panties she wore. She whimpered in spite of her determined efforts to curb the reaction.

He stood. Pressed a kiss to her cheek and turned for the door.

"No."

The single word was rough, desperate, demanding.

She couldn't let him go.

She needed him.

She wanted him.

He looked into her eyes, his as full of desire as she knew hers were. She wasn't the only one who wanted more.

"This is not what you need," he murmured.

"Last night you said we'd revisit the subject tomorrow." She reached behind her back and unhooked her bra, let it fall down her arms and onto the tile where the water swirled and rushed down the drain. "It's tomorrow."

"You're just looking for a distraction," he warned. "I don't want to be something else you'll regret."

She leaned against the wall, allowing her breasts to jut forward. "I think you missed a spot."

He grabbed the body wash and squeezed a little more onto his palm. He held her gaze as he reached for her breasts. She gasped when both hands closed over her and squeezed. He teased her nipples, leaned down and kissed her, his mouth devouring hers.

Her arms went around him, slid down his back until she encountered the waistband of his jeans. She trailed her fingers around to his fly and unfastened it. She stuck her hands inside that soft denim and ushered them slowly down his lean hips, then pushed his back against the wall this time. She kissed her way down his chest as she pushed his jeans lower and lower. When her tongue dipped into his navel, she dropped to her knees and tugged off the soaking wet jeans.

She kissed her way back up his muscled thighs, past his fully aroused penis and onto the center of his wide chest. He lifted her up, and her legs instinctively went around his waist. He shut off the water, shouldered his way out the door and headed for the bed. He lowered her onto the comforter and reached for the one thing left between them, those damned panties. He dragged the damp, strappy things down her legs, following that same path with his lips. He tossed the panties away and settled between her welcoming thighs.

As she arched her hips, his erection pressed against her, and she shuddered with need. He pulled away, apparently satisfied to taste and tease her mouth with his own.

"I can't wait any longer," she murmured between kisses. She lifted her hips into him once more.

He grinned and reached down to guide himself into her, filling her quickly and completely. She cried out with the pleasure of it. Shivers rushed through her, rippling along every muscle, pushing her toward that place of pure sensation. He held her tight, his muscled chest rubbing her breasts, grinding against her nipples until she thought she would lose her mind.

Her fingers found their way into his hair, and she relished the silky feel of it. She traced his square jaw, nipped his lips with her teeth. The rasp of his hips along her inner thighs, the stretching sensation of each thrust, the brush of his chest against her breasts…all of it had her plunging toward sensory overload.

The distant ache of climax teased her, coming nearer and nearer until the pleasure exploded inside her. One, two, three more thrusts and he came, too.

He growled as he rolled onto his side, pulling her with him, their bodies still intimately joined.

Tears burned her eyes, but she refused to cry again. She didn't know why she felt that particular urge. He was…amazing. What they'd just shared was amazing. There was no other word for it.

As if understanding, he pulled her close and whispered into her damp hair. "Please don't regret this."

"I couldn't even if I wanted to," she whispered back.

2:00 p.m.

"Where are we going?"

She'd asked him that same question four times already. "It's a surprise." Lacon grinned at her.

"Okay. I like surprises. Sometimes."

"You'll like this surprise, I promise."

He'd had to select a car from the garage. All the blood in his would just remind her of the nightmare at Hirsch and Kildare. For now, he intended to do all in his power to keep that smile on her face and that sweet laughter coming from her luscious mouth.

He'd taken her to his favorite burger joint for lunch. They'd eaten all the bad stuff: burgers, fries, shakes. He'd had her pegged for a vanilla girl, but she'd gone straight for the chocolate. He couldn't remember the last time he'd laughed so much as she'd told him stories of her and her brother's antics as kids.

She'd asked a million questions about his family and childhood, as if all he'd previously told her hadn't been nearly enough. So he'd decided to give her the grand tour—at least the one he could give without driving all the way to Texas.

He parked in front of his town house on Rockwell. She peered out the window at the two-story redbrick duplex. It wasn't as fancy as her place, but it was his home away from home, and he was comfortable here.

She whirled in the seat to face him. "Is this where you live?"

He nodded. "You want to come in?"

"Yes." She reached for the door.

He emerged, checked the street in both directions

and met her on the sidewalk. He resisted the urge to take her hand as they strolled up the walk. Six steps up to the stoop and through the common door. A small hall that had once been a glamorous foyer went left to his town house and right to his neighbor's.

As soon as he'd unlocked the door, Issy rushed in ahead of him. His gut tightened. What she thought of his place suddenly mattered way too much.

She wandered all around the reasonably spacious living room. He should probably get a rug for the hardwood, but the bare wood floors had never bothered him. His sofa and chair were big, overstuffed and comfortable. A couple of handy tables, a big-ass television and he was good to go. About the only other thing he needed was someone to curl up on that big old sofa with him.

That his gaze rested on her warned him that he was moving way too fast into personal territory. He'd been trained to avoid that dangerous deviation. He knew better. But he couldn't slow the momentum.

"I love the fireplace."

"It comes in handy on those cold Windy City nights." He joined her at the mantel where she was examining the family photos that lined it.

"Your sister is beautiful."

"Thanks. My dad insists she looks just like our mother did at that age."

Issy smiled at him and moved on to the group

photo they'd taken on Father's Day. "Wow. All you Traynor men are handsome."

A spark of jealousy burned in him. "Really?" He took the framed photo from her. "Those two?" He shook his head. "No way. I got all the looks in the family."

Another of those relaxed smiles spread across her face. He could barely breathe just watching the happiness bloom on her countenance.

"Let's see the kitchen. Do you cook as much here as you do when you're on duty at the safe house?"

"Absolutely."

He led the way through the small dining room to the kitchen. "There's a patio out back."

She walked around the kitchen, touched the cabinet doors, trailed her fingers over the counter. His mind conjured up the memory of his fingers trailing over her skin, feeling her body shiver against him… feeling her coming around him. He swallowed hard, tried to think of something witty to say.

"It's cozy." She surveyed his spice rack and the stack of cookbooks in the corner, then she touched the hand towel that hung on the oven door handle. It said Cooking Good. His sister had given it to him at Christmas. "I can tell you spend a lot of time in here."

He shrugged. "When I'm home I cook."

"Can I see upstairs?" She bit her lower lip as if she

was worried he would say no. "You've seen where I sleep."

"Sure." He gestured toward the stairs. "Make yourself at home."

She strolled past him and hurried up the stairs. He climbed a little slower, mostly because that way he got to watch the sweet sway of her hips. It wasn't like there was a lot to see up there—beyond the gorgeous woman in front of him. There were two bedrooms and one bathroom, besides the tiny half bath downstairs. She wandered from room to room, lingering in his bedroom. Soft music whispered from the clock radio.

"Nothing to see." He gestured to the bed. "Bed. Dresser and closet." He shrugged. "And one small bedside table. I leave the radio on like that all the time." The volume was turned down so low you could barely hear the music. He liked the gentle sound, like the soft roar of the ocean.

She grabbed him by the hand and pulled him toward the bed. "I want to lie here with you and listen."

"Really?"

"Yes. It's kind of silly, but I want to *feel* your space."

"Okeydokey."

He climbed onto the bed and lay down beside her. They stared at the ceiling fan going round and round, listened to the soft notes of the music filtering through the air.

"Your bed is comfy."

"Yeah."

Her hand found his, and their fingers instinctively intertwined.

The tight feeling in his chest worried him. He was liking this way too much.

The vibration in his jacket pocket alerted him to a call. He exhaled a big breath and dug the damned thing out. At least it wasn't hers. Anastasia wouldn't call him.

He stared at the number. Didn't recognize it.

"Traynor."

"Mr. Traynor, this is Chief Anthony Waller."

Lacon stilled. "How can I help you, Chief?"

"We need to have a meeting."

Surprised, Lacon asked, "What time and where?"

"Now, if possible. I've contacted Victoria. She's already en route. We're meeting near the old station house on Halsted Street in Lincoln Park. I realize it's short notice, so how quickly can you be there?"

Lacon sat up. "Half an hour."

"Bring Dr. Frasier with you. This can't wait."

"We'll be there."

Issy was sitting up now, her gaze searching his face. "What's going on?"

"Chief Waller wants a meeting. He said Victoria is already en route."

Issy finger combed her hair. “Then I guess we have to go.”

Lacon didn’t have a good feeling about this. As they moved back downstairs, he decided it would be best to contact Michaels en route to confirm this impromptu meeting. They had no control over Anastasia’s actions, but this felt wrong somehow. His instincts were sounding off.

At the front door, he hesitated. “Stay inside while I have a look around outside.”

She hugged her arms around herself. “Okay.”

He hated the fear that took the place of the happiness he’d watched light up her face until that damned phone call interrupted. She’d been through too much already. He didn’t like any of this, not one little bit.

Outside, he surveyed the street. Checked the car. All seemed as it should be. He put in a call to Ian Michaels. Got his voice mail. He left a message for Michaels to let him know what was going on with the Waller meeting. He left the location just in case.

Once Lacon felt confident there was no danger lurking nearby, he locked his place and ushered Issy out to the car. He took a few shortcuts to reach the neighborhood where the old defunct police station still stood. He’d added a little time on to what was necessary when Waller questioned him. His instincts still nagged relentlessly at him.

Something wasn’t right.

He parked behind another vehicle on the side street next to the bank across from the old police station and cut the engine. He surveyed the street in front of the old station house. So far he saw nothing unusual, but that didn't mean something unusual wouldn't come out of the woodwork like roaches after dark.

"What do we do now?" She looked at him, her eyes clearly conveying that she was worried because he was worried.

"Let's just stay in the background and see how this plays out until we hear from Michaels."

Five minutes later, an SUV arrived. Chief Waller got out and walked halfway down the block. Maybe ten seconds later a dark car, big with heavily tinted windows, eased to the curb. Waller leaned down at the rear passenger side and appeared to be talking to someone.

The vehicle was not an agency vehicle. There was no sign of Victoria or Michaels. This was definitely not right, by any stretch of the imagination.

"This is all wrong." Traynor started the car and slowly backed down the side street. When he was far enough from the intersection to avoid detection, he executed a u-turn and sped away.

"Do you think Chief Waller was trying to set us up?"

Lacon checked his rearview mirror. "I don't know,

but I didn't recognize that car as one of the agency's. I didn't see Victoria or Michaels either."

His cell vibrated and he checked the screen. This time it was Michaels. "Traynor."

Michaels confirmed his gut instinct. Victoria had not received a call from Waller. The chief had lied.

The meet was a setup.

Chapter Nine

Colby Safe House, 6:30 p.m.

Victoria had already met with Chief Connie Staten regarding Chief Waller's potential criminal activities. Marissa hated the idea of one of the top cops in the city being on Anastasia's side, but she wasn't foolish enough to believe it didn't happen. For some, money was more important than anything else, even executing their sworn duties.

"Does this mean that Anastasia knows where we are?" The idea had only just occurred to her. Her heart thumped hard against her ribs.

Lacon raised his hands in a hold-up gesture. "Right now we have no reason to believe he knows where you are. Waller was never given this address. He only knows that you're at one of the agency's safe houses. The addresses are a closely guarded secret."

"So there are others?" She relaxed the tiniest bit. This feeling of not being in control of her own destiny, of being totally at someone else's mercy, had her completely on edge. She had agreed to do this, but she hadn't expected to not be able to trust the good guys. The reality of the situation felt far graver now. Caused her to doubt herself.

"Several." He glanced around the kitchen, set his hands on his lean hips. "You up for chicken? I've mastered several mean chicken-and-rice recipes."

As unsettled as she was about this latest turn of events, she had to smile. He really was such a nice man. Whatever happened, when this was over, she hoped they could remain friends. Her body heated just standing here looking at him. She wasn't sure friends would ever be enough. But she also realized that right now she was his job—his work—and this wasn't necessarily the beginning of anything deeper.

It just felt that way.

So not smart, Issy.

"That sounds great." She pushed all the troubling thoughts away. "What can I do?"

He grinned. She loved that grin. Her heart stumbled. *Don't even go there, silly.*

"Find something green that goes well with chicken and rice."

"I think I can handle that." She went to the fridge. "Someone stocks this place whenever there's a guest?"

Or maybe he'd done the shopping, too. But no, she didn't think so. She couldn't see how he would have had the time between when she reached out to her friend Eva Bowman and when Lacon showed up at her house after William's murder.

"There's a staff that takes care of the cleaning and the shopping."

She had been surprised when they returned to find the en suite in her room spotless, the bloody clothes gone. She hoped they had thrown those clothes away because she certainly never wanted to see them again.

Her exploration of the fridge turned up kale and spinach, two of her favorites. All they needed was the right dressing for a healthy salad.

The cell in the hip pocket of her jeans vibrated, reminding her that she had nothing clean left to wear after today. This pair of jeans and the "Doctors would be lost without nurses" T-shirt were the last of the casual wear she'd packed. Obviously her idea of how long this business would take had been far too optimistic. Cutting herself some slack, she had just discovered her ex dead in the bed next to her. Her ability to think clearly had been seriously compromised. She pulled the phone from her pocket and checked the screen.

Blocked Call.

Fear swam through her veins.

"It's him."

Lacon nodded for her to answer.

The fridge started that annoying sound that warned the door had been open too long. She pushed it closed with her hip and touched the screen, accepting the call and putting it on speaker. “Frasier.”

“It’s time we met, Dr. Frasier.”

She held on to the counter, his declaration making her knees weak. “If you’ve managed to get two more of your men gravely injured, save us both some time and trouble and just shoot them.”

“Now, now, Doctor, you wound me. Sometimes it’s impossible to keep my people safe. I suppose I have far too many enemies to hope for peaceful negotiations in business.”

Marissa dropped the kale and spinach onto the counter. “If no one is in need of medical care, why are you calling?”

“As I said, I think it’s time we met in person.”

A new fear surged into her chest. She stared at Lacon. He moved his head side to side. But how was she supposed to stop Anastasia if she didn’t do as he asked? She couldn’t bring this guy down from afar. She had no choice.

“What time did you have in mind?”

Lacon looked away, but the set of his jaw told her he wasn’t happy with her decision.

“Tonight. Eight o’clock. We’ll have dinner in my home. I rarely invite anyone into my home. Consider yourself honored, Dr. Frasier. My chef is one of the finest in the city. I'm certain you will fall in love with his culinary skills."

His comment gave her pause. Did he somehow know that she had raved about Lacon's abilities in the kitchen? That was impossible. The security here was far too state-of-the-art.

Reaching for her most cavalier tone, she said, "I'll need your address."

He provided the Lincoln Park address without hesitation. "I'll see you at eight. Bring your bodyguard if you like."

The call ended. One look at her *bodyguard* and she held her breath. To say he appeared upset would be a monumental understatement.

"You know we have to do this," she ventured.

"No way in hell are we going to his house."

"Yes." She took a deep breath to bolster her waning courage. "We are. It's the only way I'll be able to get close to him. I can't stop him from a distance. I need to be closer. Close enough to connect him to a murder or some other criminal activity."

"So you've decided this is your mission in life? You're just going to take whatever risk necessary." He passed a hand over his jaw. "Not happening. I'm calling Victoria."

"Suit yourself. I'm going to get ready."

He was already making the call when she walked out. Maybe it wasn't a smart move. Anastasia could be planning to kill her. The trouble was, she couldn't keep living this way. She had a career. Was she supposed to go back to work not knowing when he would call and demand she appear and make a house call for him? How long would she have to play that game before she got close enough to find some sort of leverage to help bring him down?

She didn't want to live that way. Didn't want to follow in William's footsteps.

Peeling off the jeans and T-shirt, she went into the closet. The dress clothes she had brought for meeting Victoria would have to do. The black slacks were some of her favorites. The blouse, too. The flats were comfortable and dressy enough. She didn't actually care what this piece of shit thought of how she looked. She just wanted to get closer—close enough to learn at least one of his secrets.

She hadn't brought any makeup, which was fine by her. She rarely wore it anyway. She brushed her hair, let it fall in those wild curls that were the bane of her existence. Perfume was the last thing she'd been thinking about when she'd packed. The cherry blossom scent of the body wash still lingered on her skin. Good enough.

She'd just shut off the light and exited the en suite bath when Lacon walked into her room, the tension in the set of his shoulders like a flashing neon sign that screamed frustration.

"You're determined to do this, aren't you?"

"It's the only way I'll ever be free of him." She

clasped and unclasped her hands. "I can't stay hidden like this forever."

He dropped his head. "You're right. He's not going to stop using you until someone stops him." He lifted his gaze back to hers. "I don't know if we can count on the police to make that happen. He's a powerful guy, and the kind of money he throws around can sometimes sway even the most honorable man."

"Which means it's up to us."

"I just don't like it."

She walked over to where he stood and wrapped her arm around one of his. "I don't like it either. But I can't think of a better plan."

"I don't want you alone with him."

"I want you right beside me every minute."

"All right. Let's do this. Give me five to change clothes."

"I'll have a glass of wine while I wait."

They parted in the hallway. He went to his room and she descended the stairs. In the kitchen, she picked through the chilled white wines until she found one of her favorites. In the past couple of years, she'd become quite the expert at removing wine corks. Before it had always been William's job. Funny how so many little things changed when a marriage ended. Luckily, the cork gave her no trouble. She poured a glass and savored a long drink. Though she needed a clear head for tonight, a little fortification was in order, as well.

She had finished off the healthy serving by the time Lacon appeared at the door. Her breath caught in her throat. "Wow."

It wasn't until he grinned that she realized she had said the word out loud. Her face warmed with embarrassment.

She shook her head and confessed, "You look… *wow.*" The black trousers and the black shirt fit him like a glove. But the perfect crowning touches were the boots and the jacket. "Really nice."

"You set a high bar, Doc. You look amazing yourself."

Her blush deepened, and she felt the blood rush even harder to her cheeks. "I think maybe you have a little cabin fever, Mr. Traynor. You're delirious."

"I don't think so." He put the wine away while she rinsed her glass. His gaze settled on hers, and the doubt there was unmistakable. "Shall we go?"

She put her arm in his. "It's too late to back out now."

Maybe tonight she would learn something important to the mission without anyone having to die. That would be the best-case scenario, at any rate.

North Burling Street, 8:00 p.m.

Marissa had been to her share of mansions. The Edge administrator, Devon Pierce, lived in a gorgeous mansion out in Highland Park. It was genuinely beautiful. But this house with its manicured grounds, discreet landscape lighting, an iron fence and gate that sprawled along a full city block on Lincoln Park's most prestigious street. The term *mansion* seemed wholly inadequate.

An armed guard opened the intricate iron gate and greeted them at the sidewalk. The landscape and fountains alone probably cost more than Marissa's entire house. The home's towering front double doors opened as they climbed the limestone steps.

"Good evening, Dr. Frasier," the man dressed all in white said. He ignored Lacon. "Mr. Anastasia is waiting for you in the parlor. Directly ahead and to your left."

"Thank you." She smiled for the man, whom she decided was a butler. Did butlers even exist anymore?

"Sir, I will need your weapon," the butler said to Lacon.

He relinquished the weapon in his side holster without fanfare but kept the one in his boot. He'd told her about it on the drive here.

The entry hall was enormous, with a ceiling that soared up three floors. The winding staircase railing was black and gold, with marble steps twisting around the grand hall all the way up to the second floor and beyond. The gleaming marble floors flowed forward, changing to rich hardwood as they entered the parlor. Unlike the crisp white walls of the entry hall, the parlor walls were clad in rich mahogany paneling. A stone fireplace was surrounded by comfortable chairs in an elegant conversation grouping. In the center of the room, two sofas faced each other. An impressive chandelier hung from the soaring ceiling.

Anastasia stood at the wall of windows that looked out over the back of his urban estate. He turned to greet her, and she was surprised to find that he was not as old as she'd expected. The photos of him that Lacon had showed her were always taken from a distance, and his face was rarely clear enough to see the details. He was undeniably young and attractive. But his gray eyes were predatory, cunning. She didn't like his eyes, particularly as they roved over her as if she were his prey.

He smiled, surprising her again. "Dr. Frasier, it is a pleasure to meet you."

Before she could answer, he crossed the room, took her hand and brushed his lips across it. She barely restrained a shiver of revulsion and hoped she had managed to conceal the reaction.

"I'm sorry I can't say the same, Mr. Anastasia." She withdrew her hand from his. His touch made her feel ill.

"What would you like to drink?" He gestured to the elegant bar across the room. "Wine? A martini?"

She had to be careful to keep a clear head, but chances were if she drank, he would, as well. Then again, maybe she'd read far too many mysteries. "White wine. Thank you."

"And you, Mr. Traynor?" He looked beyond her. "Scotch? Bourbon?"

"Nothing for me."

Marissa glanced at him. Hearing his voice, though weighted with irritation, made her feel safe. He stood a few feet away, arms hanging loosely, hands clasped in front of him. He and the man pouring the drinks could not be more different. Lacon's silky blond hair and light golden brown eyes were a stark contrast to Anastasia's raven-black hair that brushed his shoulders and eyes so dark they were nearly black.

Both men were tall, but Lacon had the lean, muscular build of an athlete. Anastasia was thinner. He wore black trousers as well, but rather than a button-down shirt, he had donned a silk V-neck pullover that clung to his body like a second skin. He appeared fit, but she doubted he possessed the physical strength of the man who had made love to her last night. She shivered at the memories. This time she could not restrain the pleasant sensation.

Anastasia brought the stemmed glass of wine to her, his own tumbler of bourbon in his other hand.

She lifted the glass to her mouth, but then hesitated as she remembered that this man had ordered someone to drug her wine so she wouldn't wake up while her house was broken into and her ex-husband was murdered and left in her bed.

"It's the best." He sent a pointed look at her wine.

When she still hesitated, he nodded. "I see. You think there might be something in the wine."

Before she could answer, he took her glass and downed the contents. "Now," he licked his lips, "would you like a glass of wine?"

"I would." Only then did her heart begin to slow from its frantic race.

When he'd poured her another glass of wine, the butler who'd taken Lacon's weapon appeared and announced that dinner was served. They migrated to the equally luxurious dining room that would easily accommodate forty. The table was set for three at the end nearest yet another wall of windows.

Anastasia held her chair and then sat down at the head of the table. Lacon was seated directly across from her. Marissa felt as if she were in one of those old gangster movies.

More staff dressed in white, a woman and a man, rushed around the dining room delivering their salads and leaving cutting boards loaded with fresh bread. Water goblets were filled. Linen napkins were placed across their laps.

Anastasia wanted to know everything about her, from her childhood to her work at the Edge. He acted as if he knew nothing of her background. She knew this was a lie, but his performance as the uninformed was nothing short of award winning. He said nothing to Lacon. It was as if he wasn't in the room.

By the time dessert arrived, the tension between the two men was palpable.

Marissa stole glances at Lacon, but his full attention was on the man at the end of the table. The dessert was delicious. The raspberries and blackberries provided the perfect tart contrast to the creamy ricotta mousse with its distinct hint of orange liqueur. She nibbled at the dessert while coffee was served.

Her mind wouldn't stop with the questions. Why had Anastasia invited her here? What did he want? What did he need to prove? That he had the grandest mansion in all of Chicago? That he had a hell of a chef and a loyal staff?

Or was it that he wanted to show her he could be just another billionaire businessman?

Whatever his intent, he wasn't fooling Marissa. She knew what he was. A heartless, greedy criminal who would do anything to achieve his goal. This man had murdered William. He had killed at least two other people in the short time since she learned of his existence.

He was a monster.

ANASTASIA STOOD.

Lacon had never been so grateful for anything in his life. If he survived this night without punching the guy's face in, it would be a flat-out miracle.

This meeting, however important they had hoped it would be, had proven utterly pointless. The only thing Lacon had learned was that the bastard was seriously obsessed with Issy.

Anastasia couldn't keep his eyes off her. He took advantage of every damned opportunity to touch her. Her hand, her arm. Lacon was about ready to explode.

You have really screwed this one up, buddy.

Lacon had allowed the relationship with Issy to become personal. Images of last night flickered through him, reminding him that he'd made a serious mistake. But he couldn't call what he'd felt a mistake. It wasn't just sex…it was more. Still, protecting her had to be his top priority. Nothing else could get in the way.

"I'd like to show you something," Anastasia said to Issy.

Fury eating at him, Lacon trailed behind the two as they exited the house through the French doors that lined the dining room. A terrace flanked the back of the house. Overhead, a balcony ran that same length. Down the steps was a reflecting pool and fountain, as well as a large gazebo that covered an outdoor living room. The property was bordered with thick shrubs and trees, giving more privacy than he would have expected to find in such an urban setting.

Anastasia appeared to be headed for the garage. Like the one at the Colby safe house, the garage was a six-bay structure that faced the street running behind the house. Considering the property covered an entire city block, there could potentially be street access on all four sides. Lacon had only spotted this one access.

Between the gardens and the garage was a carriage house. Anastasia placed his hand at the small of Issy's back and ushered her in the direction of the carriage house. Fury exploded deep in Lacon's gut.

Damn it. Where was his objectivity when he needed it?

Anastasia entered the code that unlocked the door and pushed it inward. Lacon stepped ahead of Issy. "I need to have a look first."

Anastasia gestured to the door. "I have premiere security, but by all means, be my guest."

Rather than a guesthouse as he'd expected, the carriage house was like a small medical clinic. He checked the other doors. One led to living quarters and the other to a small private courtyard.

Lacon gestured for Issy to come on in, then he stepped aside to observe. He had a feeling he wasn't going to like what came next.

"This is the clinic I had prepared in anticipation of taking on a private physician as part of my staff."

Issy wandered around the room. Lacon was no doctor, but he'd never seen a better-equipped clinic. Not surprising, really, since Anastasia was megarich. *Bastard.*

The other thing Lacon had recognized tonight was the sheer jealousy he felt every single time Anastasia looked at her, much less touched her. He shook his head, frustrated with himself.

"This is pretty incredible," Issy admitted.

Lacon reminded himself she was playing along, but he still didn't like her positive reaction.

"This is where you will work." Anastasia shook his head. "No more rushing to locations where what you need might not be available. I've put you through a great deal this week, but I needed to know I could count on you—that you could handle the demands of my business. I have no doubts now. You possess the necessary skills, and you are beautiful. You're exactly what I've been looking for."

"This is all very nice," she said, drawing Lacon from his fixation with beating the guy to a bloody pulp. "But I already have a position that means a great deal to me. The people, the facility—I can't walk away from either."

Lacon didn't miss the flash of anger in the other man's cold eyes.

"You work for me now," he reminded her. "Going back to the way your life once was isn't possible, so don't waste your time fighting the inevitable. This is where you will work."

Issy cocked her head and studied him a moment. "What's in it for me? Contrary to what you obviously believe, I don't live my life for you or to serve your every whim."

"I thought you understood the nature of our relationship, Issy."

Who the hell gave him permission to call her Issy? Lacon clenched his teeth, kept his mouth shut. His fingers curled into fists.

"What is our relationship?" She took a step toward Anastasia. Lacon tensed. "You drugged me, murdered my ex-husband and left him in my bed, and you think that constitutes a relationship? Please, you must know that I can't just forget those two ugly facts. You've put me in an untenable position."

Anastasia's jaw worked a second before he spoke. "Bauer left me no choice. He should have known better than to double-cross a man like me. He made a very bad decision and he paid the price."

"A lapse in judgment, for sure," she agreed. "I've done my research, Mr. Anastasia. I'm aware of the kind of man you are."

"Vito," he reminded her. At some point over dinner, he'd urged her to call him Vito. "What has your research told you?"

"The most lucrative part of your business is done behind the scenes. But then there's the legitimate business you operate. You have many powerful friends and allies. How would it look to them if they learned you had hired a murder suspect? Until this business with William is cleared up, I have to face the very real possibility that I could be charged with murder."

"You needn't worry. I will clear up any questions related to your involvement in that unsavory business immediately. You'll receive the call tomorrow."

Issy seemed uncertain how to respond. Then she went for the jugular. "You murdered the man I once loved. How can you expect me to pretend that didn't happen?"

He stepped nearer to her, and Lacon prepared to step between them.

"William Bauer killed himself. He understood when he took matters into his own hands what he was doing." Anastasia studied her for one seemingly endless moment. "Would you be so quick to jump to your ex-husband's defense if you knew that he spoke often of how he hated you? Of how he wished you dead?"

She blinked. Lacon flinched.

"I don't believe you." She shook her head. "We didn't get along and he was angry that I pressed charges—"

"He hated you. He asked me to have you killed, but I refused."

The color drained from her face. "What are you talking about?"

"He wanted you dead because he knew you hadn't changed your will or your insurance policies. All that was yours would be his and, in time, he would regain his license to practice medicine. He couldn't risk killing you himself." Anastasia frowned. "I did worry toward the end that he might snap and attempt to harm you."

"*You* worried about me?" Disbelief underscored her tone.

Lacon was proud of her. He'd just thought the same thing.

"I did. When I learned of William's latest bad decision, I decided it would be in both our best interests to put an end to his plotting."

"So you drugged me and had him killed—and put in my bed—in an effort to protect me." She laughed. "That's rich, Vito, but I'm not buying it."

Lacon resisted the urge to smile.

"Well, there was the matter of getting your attention and, of course, your cooperation."

"Thank you for dinner and the tour of your home." She turned away from him and strode toward the door.

Lacon hesitated going after her just so he could see the man's reaction when he realized she was actually leaving.

Outrage streaked across the bastard's face. "No one walks away from me."

Lacon moved toward her. She stood at the door now, staring back at the man who had spoken.

"If you want me to work for you," she said, "then you need to make it worth my while. The police have been all over me, as a murder suspect and as a potential way to get to you."

Renewed tension slid through Lacon.

"The police have asked you to be their eyes and ears against me?"

"They have."

Lacon decided she would make a damned good detective. She was aware that if Waller was the leak in the department, then Anastasia already knew this. His respect for her increased exponentially.

"And what did you do in response to this request?"

She shrugged. "I heard them out. I figured maybe if I helped them, they might stop trying to prove I had anything to do with my ex's death."

Anastasia waited for her to go on, his gaze narrowed.

"But then I realized they were just using me." She shook her head. "I was used by my ex—I'm not going to be used by anyone else. The next time they asked for a meeting, I blew them off."

A smile cut across the bastard's face. "I will pay you three times your current salary if you come to work for me. The benefits," he said the word so salaciously Lacon wanted to puke, "will be immeasurable."

"I'll think about it." She turned back to the door, but then hesitated again. "Just one thing." She gestured to Lacon. "He goes where I go."

Anastasia sized him up again, this time more slowly. "I have no issue with that request. I'm certain he would be an asset to me, as well."

Lacon was relatively certain from his tone that he didn't mean as a member of his security team.

Issy shook her head. "Sorry. He's all mine. You can look, but no touching."

Another of those sick smiles lit the other man's face. "As you wish."

She held the other man's gaze as if she might say more. Lacon wanted to urge her out the door, but she'd done a damned good job of handling the situation so far. He wasn't about to mess with her momentum.

"How am I supposed to trust you, Vito?" She folded her arms over her chest. "First you regale me with stories of how often William spoke of me. You mentioned that he said I loved my patients. Now you want me to believe that he hated me. Wanted me dead."

Anastasia moved closer to her. Renewed tension coiled in Lacon.

"He spoke of you often, but none of it was good. It was his obsession with hating you that led me to see for myself all that you were. William Bauer was a fool. A liar and a fool."

Issy ignored his thinly veiled compliment. "Just one more question."

Anastasia lifted his eyebrows in inquiry.

"Why me? There are lots of talented doctors in this city. Why does it have to be me?"

"All these months I found myself watching you,

learning about you. You intrigue me, Dr. Marissa Frasier. It must be you. It cannot be anyone else. You have forty-eight hours to make your decision."

The stare-off lasted another ten seconds before she walked out the door.

Lacon followed her without a backward glance. He was more than ready to get out of this snake den.

At the front door, the gray-haired man in the white suit returned his weapon and bid them a good evening. The same guard opened the gate at the street for them to pass, then closed and locked it. Lacon checked the street and his car before allowing Issy to get inside.

He didn't breathe easy until they were a mile or so away from Anastasia's compound.

"You okay?" He glanced at her, wished he could see her face better, but it was too dark.

"I'm good. I just need to get back to the house so I can take another shower. I feel dirty having breathed the same air as that scumbag."

Lacon laughed. That was the best line he'd heard all night.

Chapter Ten

"We have a tail."

Marissa clutched the armrest and glanced at Lacon. "You think it's Anastasia's men?" Like she had to ask. Her stomach was still churning from the time spent with the man. The things she had read about him in the research Lacon had shown her sickened her. What kind of man could do those things?

She wasn't naive. The world could be a dangerous place. She knew men like Vito Anastasia existed. She saw the harm one human could wreak upon another in the ER more often than she would like.

But somehow it felt more oppressive and far more terrifying when the horrors came from a person who looked so normal…so polished and who presented himself so graciously.

"That would be my guess," he said in answer to her question. "He wants us to know there's no escaping his reach."

Marissa felt suddenly cold. She hugged her arms

around her body. "I wanted to do this. I hoped I could get us one step closer to accomplishing the goal, but all I did was open up another door in this maze of insanity. I don't see how we can ever hope to stop him. He's… I…" She sighed. "I failed."

"You did great, Issy. It was the right decision. I was the one who wasn't thinking clearly."

She didn't question what he meant by the statement. She had to admit that having him say as much made her feel better about the outcome of tonight. Not only had she not learned anything usable, now she was in deeper trouble than before. She had forty-eight hours to give the bastard a response to his demand.

"What do we do about whoever is following us?"

He reached into his pocket and withdrew his cell. "Traynor."

Marissa chewed her lips as she waited for him to finish the call. When he'd tucked the phone back into his pocket, he said, "Michaels says our tail is an unmarked cop car."

"Mr. Michaels is following us, too?"

"I never go into a risky situation without backup."

She'd wondered why he caved so easily in the end about the dinner invitation. "So what do we do about the cop following us?"

"Maybe I'll just have a talk with him and see what it is they want. Brace yourself."

She pushed back into the seat, braced one hand on

the armrest, the other on the dash. He hit the brakes, bringing the car to a rubber-burning, tire-squealing abrupt halt.

Behind them more tires squealed. The car charged up so close their headlights disappeared from the rearview mirror. Marissa held her breath. When there was no crash, she relaxed. The car hadn't slammed into theirs. Thank God.

A car door slammed hard. Whoever was in the car—presumably a cop—was getting out. Lacon drew his weapon, held it on his lap.

There was a knock at his window, followed by a detective's shield being pressed against the glass, and Marissa sagged with relief.

Lacon powered down his window. "What can I do for you, Detective?"

The man leaned down and peered into the car. *Detective Nader.* He glared at them. "We need to have a conference, Mr. Traynor."

We? Only then did Marissa realize a man was standing outside her door, too.

"There's a coffee shop over on Clark that's still open," Lacon suggested. "We'll meet you there." He hit the accelerator and took off, leaving the two detectives standing on the street in the dark.

"Do you think they're involved, like Waller?" She put her hand to her chest and ordered her heart to stop its pounding. She needed to calm down.

"I don't know, but we'll play along and see what we find out."

The short drive to the coffee shop allowed Marissa to collect herself. Whatever Nader and Watts wanted, she needed to at least appear calm. No doubt they had followed them from Anastasia's place. Should she tell them what she'd seen so far? She couldn't be sure.

When Lacon parked, she asked, "Will Michaels be watching?"

"He will, and then he'll follow us back to the safe house."

Marissa was impressed with the Colby Agency all over again. She was immensely grateful Eva had referred her to them.

She considered Lacon's profile. She was grateful for the recommendation and a whole lot more. Whatever happened when this was over, this man had shown her that she could feel again…that she should trust herself completely. She hadn't done that in a long time.

Lacon Traynor was one of those guys that girls dreamed about meeting. When it came to knights in shining armor, he was the real deal. The thought made her smile.

The coffee shop was quiet. Only a handful of patrons were scattered around the small dining area. Lacon ordered two black coffees and found them a table as far away from the few customers as possible. Nader and Watts were given coffee on the house for being members of Chicago PD. They wove through the tables and joined them. Both looked as weary as Marissa felt. Their long day showed in their rumpled suits and bleary eyes. She really hoped these two could be trusted and weren't on Anastasia's payroll.

"You two have a hot date tonight?" Nader asked as he settled into a chair.

"I'm sure you know where we were," Lacon said. "Whatever you have to say, say it. No games. We're tired of games. Especially games initiated by the police."

"We just wanted to give you an update." Nader sipped his coffee.

"Yeah," Watts echoed, "we thought you might want to know."

Lacon glanced at the clock on the wall. "It's after eleven at night—whatever you need to tell us couldn't have waited until morning?"

Watts shrugged. "It isn't like we got you out of bed." He sent a knowing glance at Marissa. "You don't mind hearing news about your late husband, do you, Doctor?"

Marissa fisted her hands together in her lap so no one would see them shaking. "What news?"

"He was drugged with the same one used on you," Nader announced.

An ache pierced her chest. "So he was unconscious when he was shot?"

Watts nodded. "Most likely."

Marissa was glad he hadn't suffered. "So, are you ruling me out as a suspect?" Anastasia's promise reverberated inside her, but she doubted he could possibly work that fast. This new development had to be coincidence. Or maybe Anastasia had already heard what the police had learned, and that was why he'd offered to get her name cleared. She had never met such a cunning monster.

"Well, it's not quite that simple," Nader said. "We have a few more things to work out, but you definitely dropped considerably down our short list."

That was something. She nodded but didn't go so far as to say thank you.

"I do have one question." Nader leaned back in his chair. "Why would you be visiting Anastasia at his home? The only people we see going in and out of his private residence are those closely associated with him. This has been nagging at me all evening, Dr. Frasier. You see," he leaned forward once more, propped his arms on the table, "I really want to believe you're one of the good ones, but this looks awfully suspicious."

She met Lacon's gaze. How did she answer that question? She hoped he had picked up on how lost she was here.

"Gentlemen—" Lacon leaned into the table as Nader had "—our mutual enemy invited Dr. Frasier for dinner. Is there a law against having dinner?"

Watts snickered. "Depends upon who you're dining with."

Lacon looked from one to the other. "You see, we're receiving mixed signals from the folks in your department. Maybe you expect us to tell you all our secrets and what we were doing tonight, but I'm afraid we just can't trust you on that level. Dr. Frasier's protection is my top priority."

"What mixed signals?" Nader demanded in a furious whisper.

"Well—" Lacon leaned even closer to him "—you might want to ask Chief Waller about that."

Nader and Watts exchanged a look. "All right." Nader glanced around the shop. "Lookie here. Me and Watts, we know there's trouble in the department where Anastasia is concerned, but we're not part of that trouble. In fact, we don't know anyone who is."

"But what we do know—" Watts joined the huddle "—is that someone way higher up the food chain is, as they say, thick as thieves with him."

Marissa wanted to just blurt out all that she knew. It would be so easy to trust them and tell them everything she and Lacon suspected so far, but Chief Staten had instructed Victoria to pass along the advice that Lacon and Marissa should not trust anyone but her. At least until she figured this out. Marissa felt certain the woman was still grappling with the idea that a man at Waller's level could be bought.

"Well," Lacon said, "we appreciate that you fellows are good cops, but you've got to understand our position. We're just trying to stay alive."

Nader gave a nod. "I can understand that. I'm just saying that if you happen to learn something we need to know, you can feel comfortable calling us." He looked to Marissa then. "You have our number."

"I do." There was a card somewhere in her purse.

"The bottom line is," Watts said, "someone—and we all know who that someone likely is—broke into your home, drugged you and your ex, then put him in your bed and killed him. I'm just a little confused as to why you'd want to break bread with the man and not give us a heads-up."

Marissa held the man's gaze, anger rushing into her throat. How dare these two accuse her of such a thing when she was only doing what she believed she had to do?

"Sometimes..." She hesitated to steady her voice.

"Sometimes," Lacon agreed, "you do what you have to do because no one else can do it for you."

Nader nodded somberly. "I would just hate to see you follow the same path your ex followed. It'd be a shame for that to happen."

"I can guarantee you both," Lacon assured, "that I'm not going to allow Dr. Frasier to get hurt."

Marissa shook her head. "You shouldn't worry about me, Detective. I have no plans to emulate any of the mistakes my ex-husband made in the final years of his life."

Nader withdrew his cell phone. “We found a couple of guys in a Dumpster over off Kildare. We thought one or both might be connected to your dinner date. Have you seen either one of these men before?”

Lacon stared at the screen before Nader turned it toward Marissa and showed her first one and then another photo. Fear tightened her throat. The first had been the man with the two gunshot wounds that she hadn’t been able to save. The other was the man who’d suffered the laceration across his abdomen—the one who’d been alive when Anastasia’s men had taken him from that storeroom.

Lacon pushed back his chair and stood. “Good night, gentlemen.”

Marissa couldn’t take her eyes from the screen even as Lacon rounded the table and stood behind her chair, waiting for her to follow his lead. A dozen things she could have said whirled in her head as she rose from her chair, her legs shaky, but none of those things felt right. Instead, she turned and walked out of the coffee shop with Lacon.

He was the only person she trusted in all this.

Colby Safe House, Monday, July 2, 12:50 a.m.

LACON PLACED HIS weapon on the bedside table. He couldn’t remember the last time he’d been this pissed off. He shouldered out of his jacket and pitched it on a chair.

He'd given Michaels an update on the drive back. Like Lacon, the senior investigator couldn't get right with the timing of the visit from the detectives. How the hell could they have known about the invitation from Anastasia? It wasn't like they could have followed them from the safe house.

There was always the chance that Nader and Watts had made it a personal mission to watch Anastasia as often as their work schedule would allow. They obviously understood that Bauer's death was on Anastasia, not to mention a truckload of other murders.

Both men from the scene at the old store were dead. At least now Lacon understood why the tracking device he'd tucked in the one guy's pocket had never left the neighborhood. Nader had shown them the photos of the bodies. Anastasia's men had apparently executed the man with the superficial knife wound.

Marissa had been devastated all over again by the photos. He'd watched the tears fill her eyes before she closed herself in her room. For that and so many other things, he wanted to rip Anastasia's arms from his body and beat him to death with them. Even a slow, torturous death wouldn't come close to covering what Anastasia deserved.

"Son of a bitch." He yanked his shirt free of his

jeans and started unbuttoning it. He wanted to hurt Vito Anastasia like he'd never wanted to hurt anyone before. Lacon understood that he had crossed the line so far he couldn't even see it anymore, much less get back to the other side. If he messed up and Issy got hurt…

"Idiot." Hopping on one foot, he dragged off a boot, tossed it aside. He pulled his backup piece from the other boot, left it on the bedside table and tugged off the other boot the same way. One by one, he peeled off his socks and flung them at the chair.

He exhaled a big breath wrought with frustration and reached for his fly. A knock at the door stopped him in the middle of the task.

One, two, three—he counted to five, reminded himself of his duty in all this, and ordered his body to relax before crossing the room. At the door he stood there, mentally repeating the words—*This is a case. She is a client. The agency's client.* His job was to protect her. Not take her to bed. Not get all tangled up emotionally with her.

Don't screw this up any further.

He opened the door, and she stood there in a T-shirt and nothing else—at least nothing else he could see—staring up at him. "I can't sleep."

"Would you like a glass of wine? Maybe a vodka on the rocks?" He would be more than happy with either one or both. Despite his best efforts, his gaze slid down her body, along those long legs and back up to the nipples jutting against the thin fabric of the T-shirt. He was pretty sure a whole bottle of vodka couldn't quench his thirst right now, or keep him from going any stupider than he'd already gone.

You have so screwed this up.

She shook her head and a tear slid down one cheek.

Oh hell. He pulled her into his arms and held her tight against him. The feel of her soft cheek against his chest made him weak as a kitten.

Damn. Damn. Damn.

"Hey now. We'll get you through this. It might take a little more time, but I'll keep you safe until we do."

She turned her face up to his. "I trust you completely. You're the only person I can trust." Another tear trekked down her cheek.

Holy hell, he was in trouble here. He swallowed back the warning he probably should have given her—*Don't trust me at the moment.* He couldn't even trust himself right now.

"Let's go downstairs and get you a nightcap. That'll help you sleep better."

She shook her head. "I don't want anything to drink."

He held his breath, his heart pounding so hard he was certain she felt the effect she was having on him.

"I want *you*."

"Issy."

She went up on her tiptoes and kissed his mouth. He froze. Told himself to resist. Warned himself not to take advantage of her vulnerability.

One soft hand slid inside his jeans. He growled. "Whoa, now."

She ignored him, her fingers reaching and finding his dick that was hard as a rock. He was doomed. She squeezed him. He shuddered. "Issy."

Her mouth latched on to his right nipple. She sucked hard. He blinked repeatedly. Struggled to get air into his lungs. With every ounce of willpower he possessed, he pulled her away, those warm fingers slipping away from his dick.

"You're killing me here."

Her green eyes sparkled with desire. "You're an adult. I'm an adult. I don't see the problem." She rested her palms against his chest, and his entire body reacted.

"My objectivity is already compromised," he confessed. "I can't risk making a mistake with your safety."

She shook her head. "I don't understand. Are you saying because you got upset every time Anastasia touched me or stood too close to me that your reaction was a bad thing?"

Irritation—at himself—spiked inside him. "Yeah. That's what I'm saying."

"I see." Her hands fell away from him, but her

gaze locked on his. “I’ll need the number for that Ian Michaels guy who serves as your backup.”

A frown tugged at his brow. “Why do you need his number?” He’d be happy to give it to her and all but…why?

“Because you’re fired.” She braced her hands on her hips. “If you feel compromised by this—” she gestured from her to him “—then you’re fired.”

He had to admit he hadn’t expected that reaction. “I’ll call him right now, if that’s what you want.”

He felt for his phone, remembered that it was in the pocket of his jacket. His hands fell to his sides, mostly because he suddenly felt sick to his stomach. “You really want to fire me?”

“No, Lacon. I want to make love with you, but you feel that would compromise you even more and—”

He hushed her with his mouth. Her arms went around his neck and he lifted her into his arms. He kicked the door shut and carried her to the bed. His mind was on fire, his body aching for her. She’d bested him and there was nothing he could do to stop this rush toward crash and burn.

He wanted her.

All of her. Now. This minute. He pulled off her T-shirt, lost his breath at the sight of her naked body. “Man alive.” She was so beautiful.

She came up on her knees, matching his stance. “First, I just want to touch you.”

Taking her time, she touched his face, traced the

line of his jaw, the hollows of his eyes, the shape of his lips. When he could move, he did the same, touching her face, memorizing every beautiful detail. His fingers toyed with the shell of her ears, tugged at those lush red curls. They traced each other's throats. Shoulders. Arms. Fingers. They held their hands up, palm to palm, her creamy-white skin against his rougher tanned skin. Just touching her overwhelmed him.

"My turn," he whispered.

He backed off the bed, shucked his jeans and then returned to her. He ushered her down onto the comforter and learned the rest of her body all over again. His mouth traced a path over her breasts. He sucked each nipple until she begged him to finish. Her body writhed beneath his touch as he kissed his way down her flat belly and to that sweet spot between her soft thighs.

He made her come with his tongue, then he did it again with his fingers. Every part of him was hard with need, and she was everything he needed.

"No more," she murmured. "I want you inside me."

He moved into position, nudged into her hot, wet opening just an inch or two then he held still and watched her come a third time.

When she was done, he got started, pushing all the way inside, making her scream his name.

He brought her to the edge once more, then he

sat back on his heels, pulling her with him, forcing himself deeper inside her. She gasped, those pink lips damp from their kisses, her green eyes glazed with pleasure. He rocked her back and forth until she found that instinctive rhythm in this new position. When those sweet muscles deep inside her tightened on him again, he bent forward and lost himself to the final thrusts that would take him over that edge with her.

When they had caught their breath, he held her tight. Never wanted to let go.

Chapter Eleven

9:30 a.m.

Using Lacon's sculpted chest as her pillow, Marissa propped her chin on her hands and smiled at him. "I want to hear more."

He laughed. She felt it rumble through his chest. She loved the sound of his laugh.

"My sister is going to be completely embarrassed about all the stories I've told." He stroked her hair. "She has kids of her own now. She'll swear to you that she never participated in any of those sneaky pranks."

His words tugged at something deep in Marissa's chest. It sounded as if he expected that she would meet his family. No matter how very often she reminded herself that this time was not real, not a foreshadowing of a future together, some part of her simply refused to accept it. Yet the rest of her fully understood that this was only a shared moment trapped between tragedy and uncertainty. Survival was encoded in human DNA, the mind programmed to sort through and to find the most optimistic possibilities and to take them.

She propped a smile into place. “You have my word. I will never tell.”

He cupped her face, his thumb sliding across her cheek, his gaze serious now. “You are so beautiful.”

They’d gotten up at three this morning and eaten, then they’d come back to bed and made love again. And again after that. They’d fallen asleep in each other’s arms. He’d made breakfast around seven, and then they’d ended up back in his bed again. Maybe they would spend the day here hiding from the world.

Tomorrow was soon enough to face reality.

“You make me feel beautiful.”

He pulled her upward, drawing her mouth to his. He tasted like rich coffee and the sweet jam he’d spread on his toast. Her hands rested on his hot skin, and her body relaxed along the length of his.

His cell phone rattled on the table next to his side of the bed. He groaned.

She wanted to tell him not to answer it because she wasn’t ready to let go of this moment, but she rolled onto her back instead and closed her eyes against the intrusion.

“Traynor.” He listened for a bit. “You’re sure about that?” More listening. “Glad to hear it.” A few seconds more of his silence, and then the indistinct murmur of the caller's voice. "All right. Thank you."

She held her breath as he tossed the phone back onto the table.

"That was Detective Nader."

Marissa sat up. Feeling naked at the mention of the detective's name, she pulled her knees to her chest to cover her bare breasts. "Did he have news?"

Lacon trailed a finger down her leg, drew a circle around her ankle. "He did." His gaze met hers. "The prints of the two guys they found in the Dumpster came up a match to the ones in your bedroom. So you're no longer a suspect in Bauer's murder. They're now looking to some element of organized crime—considering the two dead thugs are known players."

"We can connect those two to Anastasia." Hope bloomed in her chest. "We can take him down."

Lacon sighed. "I wish it were that easy. We can tell the police what we saw, what we did. We can tell them it was Anastasia who told you to do it. But we can't prove it. If the goal is to take him down, we need evidence."

He was right. Damn it. At least one part of the nightmare was over. Yet the relief she had expected would not come. The worry on Lacon's face told her he wasn't relieved either. The fact that she had tried to help those two made her angry. They had drugged her and killed her husband, and she'd felt bad she couldn't save them. She wanted to be glad they were dead but she couldn't bring herself to have so little regard for human life. What she understood with complete certainty was that those two men had been sacrificed.

She hated Vito Anastasia.

"Anastasia handed the police those two men to keep his promise to me."

Lacon nodded. "He sacrificed them to prove a point to you."

She pressed her forehead to her knees and fought back the damned tears. She was sick of crying. Sick of feeling the guilt for things out of her control. "I want to be grateful they're dead. I want to feel good about it. What kind of person does that make me?"

"This isn't your fault, Issy. What you're experiencing is your response to the perfectly orchestrated machinations of an egomaniac. You are the victim, not those two thugs who chose their own destiny."

She lifted her head and met his gaze once more. "How will I ever be free of him?"

He didn't respond, because they both knew the answer.

The only way to stop a man like Anastasia was to kill him.

Hampden Court, Noon

THE ONE UPSIDE to the news from the detectives was that her home had been released from evidence. The exterior signs that it had been a crime scene were now gone. No more yellow tape, no red warning bulletin taped to the door. But inside was a whole different story.

Dust from the search for fingerprints was everywhere. Drawers and shelves were disorganized from the rummaging of the police. Upstairs, the sheets from her bed and the pillows had been taken to the lab, so the bare mattress with its glaring round bloodstain was all that remained of where she had slept her last night in her home.

“We can call someone to remove the mattress and have a new one delivered,” Lacon offered. “Pillows, too. Just tell me whether you want soft or firm.”

She nodded. “That would be good. Soft. Definitely soft.”

He checked the brand of her mattress, did a quick search on Google and made the calls. She wandered around the room, surveying her things as if they were foreign objects. It didn’t feel like home anymore. How would she live here again?

“There’s a service we use frequently that can clean everything up for you,” he offered once his other calls were complete.

“No.” She shook her head. “I’ll do it.”

She didn’t want anyone else here, touching her things. If there was any possibility of her ever feeling at home again in this place, the effort had to start somewhere.

"Sounds like we have our work cut out for us." He gave her a wink. "I can handle myself surprisingly well with a mop."

"I think maybe I'll have to see that one to believe it," she teased.

Downstairs, they raided the laundry room for supplies. When Lacon pulled on a pair of plastic gloves that went halfway up his forearms, she had to laugh.

"You know," he said, ignoring her, "after my mother died, my sister and I usually got stuck with the housekeeping chores." He shrugged. "We were the youngest. My older brothers were needed in the barn or the pastures. Doing all the fun stuff."

"You looking for sympathy, tough guy?"

"No, ma'am." He gave her another of those winks that made her want to smile despite this awful mess.

"Where do you want to start?" She hefted her bucket of supplies. "While you tell me about your terrible childhood, I mean."

He pointed up. "Did you ever have to wash dishes for a whole crew of ranch hands?" He shook his head. "Not a walk in the park."

"My mother," Marissa explained as they trudged up the stairs, "was a throwback housewife from the fifties. She wore the apron and made cookies every day. Whatever shopping needed to be done, she took care of it while I was at school. Whenever I was home, she was home. The only exception was if the school needed her."

"Mine was the same way until she got sick."

At the top of the stairs, Marissa waited until he stood in front of her. "That must have been really hard. Kids need their mothers, even tough little boys."

One corner of his sexy mouth hitched up. "You have got to stop tempting me, Dr. Marissa Frasier."

Despite the fact that he smiled, she heard the sadness in his voice. He was right. This was a case. She was his job. If they were lucky, it would be over soon. She shouldn't keep prying into his personal life. In a few days he would be long gone.

And then the real hurt would come.

A glutton for punishment, Marissa nudged him into telling her more stories of his childhood while they cleaned. His stories kept her mind off the one currently unfolding in her life. She could not recall ever having seen a man more handsome in yellow plastic gloves and brandishing a bottle of furniture polish.

"Now, you're prodding all these stories out of me," he said as they settled in the kitchen for a late lunch. "When am I going to hear more about your childhood? You and your brother must have had plenty of adventures."

She smiled as she nibbled a cracker. The bread had expired so they had to make do with crackers and cheese. "I was the good girl. Never got into trouble at home or at school."

His gaze narrowed. "I find that difficult to believe."

"It's true. I spent all my time keeping my little brother out of trouble."

"No slipping out of the house with your friends after your parents were in bed, or sneaking a beer when no one was looking?"

"Nope. My brother did all those things, but not me. I was too busy studying and watching out for him."

"Is that why you stayed with Bauer as long as you did?"

He asked the question so casually, in between bites of cheese. "He was nice. Always in need of a study partner. I never thought about it that way, but I suppose the relationship felt comfortable because I was taking care of him the way I had my brother."

"He never took care of you?" Lacon searched her eyes, as if the answer were immensely important to him.

"Maybe." She shrugged. "In his own way. Not with romance, per se, no flowers or chocolates or spontaneous dates. But at one time we enjoyed talking about work."

Lacon's expression was pained. "He didn't take care of you, Issy. You deserved a lot better then, and you do now."

"My brother told me that from the moment I announced William and I were getting married." She shrugged. "I didn't listen because it felt good *enough*, and there just wasn't time to do better. I was so busy, it was easier to take what was right in front of me than to try to find time to look for something different."

He tucked a wisp of hair behind her ear. "Life gets in the way sometimes."

"I would never have imagined he would do the things he's done the past two years. I thought I knew him." She shook her head. "I guess I really didn't." That was the saddest truth of all.

"Some people are good at hiding the blackness that lurks in their soul."

He was right. She had beaten herself up plenty of times for the bad decisions she'd made with William. It was time to get past those mistakes and look to the future. And she sincerely hoped this man would be a part of her future.

His turn to talk about the more painful part of his past. "What was your fiancée like?"

He ate the last cracker on his plate, seemed to mull over her question. When he'd washed it down with the grape juice that was all she had in the house, he said, "She was kind and sweet. Pretty." He smiled. "My boss at the bonding agency where I worked warned me not to get too attached. He knew how much I loved people projects."

His words disrupted the rhythm of her heart. "People projects?"

He shrugged. "I was always helping someone. A beggar who lived on the street. A kid who just needed a father figure. A woman whose husband abused her. It was like my hobby. Helping folks is a good thing but I didn't stop at helping. I had to get emotionally involved. Attached, my sister called it. Sherry—that was her name, my fiancée—we got so tangled up with each other, I couldn't see my hand in front of my face. I should have realized what that bastard would do the first chance he got. I knew his kind. But I was blinded by love—the idea of it anyway. She died, and I will carry that burden to my grave. I should have paid better attention."

Marissa felt as if she'd been slapped in the face. He could be describing their relationship to this point—or whatever it was. She felt ill. She reached for her water and tried to dampen her parched throat.

"I was young," he went on, seemingly oblivious to her shock. "I didn't recognize the difference between infatuation and love, and the need to protect someone versus the need to be with someone."

She tried to think of something to say, but no words would come.

"I have never allowed myself to get personally involved with work again." He set down his glass and looked directly at her. "Until now."

Somehow she forced the words out around the lump in her throat. "We're both experienced adults. This isn't the same."

"No." He stared so intently at her that she ached with the weight of it. "It's not the same."

The doorbell echoed through the house. She

blinked away the damned tears that crowded into her eyes. How foolish had she been? She'd allowed her feelings to go unchecked. William's death had made her vulnerable. Lacon had tried to warn her but she hadn't listened.

He stood, drew the weapon from his waistband at the small of his back. "Stay put. I'll see who it is."

When he'd headed for the door, Marissa closed her eyes and put her shaking hands over her mouth to hold back a sob. She was a mess. Her life was a mess. A great deal of the fallout bombarding her just now was William's fault, but *this*—this emotional entanglement—was hers alone. She had no one to blame but herself.

She drew in a deep breath. She was no little girl, no young woman so involved in her career she couldn't think straight. She was a grown woman, a physician. Acting like a foolish jilted girl would be ridiculous. What she and Lacon shared was sex, mutual need. Nothing more. It was perfectly healthy to enjoy sex between consenting adults. This did not have to be complicated for either of them. His attention and tenderness had helped her get through this unspeakably difficult time. It wasn't a big deal.

Keep telling yourself that, Issy.

Lacon was suddenly standing in front of her. The abrupt pounding at her door made her jump. "It's Anastasia."

Her heart swelled into her throat. "Your car is out front. He knows we're here."

He nodded. "Stay out of sight. I'll talk to him."

She nodded and went through the kitchen to the laundry room. She kept the door open a crack so she could hear.

A few seconds later she heard Lacon say, "What can I do for you?"

The strength in his voice warmed her. All else aside, she was so grateful to have him standing between her and Anastasia. He was a good man. A loyal man. Tears burned her eyes again and she blinked them back. Whatever happened in the future, she was immensely thankful for this time with him. For his strength, his honesty and every single moment of the rest.

"I'd like to speak with Marissa."

The other man's voice made her shudder with revulsion.

"She's not available at this time," Lacon said.

Marissa held her breath, hoped he would leave.

"I'll wait."

There were footsteps and then the unmistakable squeak of leather. He was staying. Damn him.

"I think maybe you didn't hear me," Lacon said. "She's not available, now or later. You should go before I get frustrated."

Marissa pressed her hand more firmly over her mouth. The silence terrified her.

"I'm certain you've misunderstood me," Anastasia countered. "I will wait to see her. If you take issue with that, then you may sort it out with my associates."

How many did he have with him?

"Would you like to step outside, Mr. Traynor?"

Another voice. Male. Hard.

Enough.

Marissa opened the door and walked back through the kitchen and into the living room. Two men hovered around Lacon. Anastasia sat on the sofa.

"I'm a little busy," she said to the man in the sleek black suit now staring at her. "The police left my house in a mess. I won't feel at home until everything's back in order. Perhaps we can visit another time, Mr. Anastasia."

"Vito," he reminded her as he stood. "The reason I stopped by won't take long."

Lacon pushed between the two thugs and came to her side.

Anastasia glanced at him as he moved ever closer to Marissa. "I thought you might want to thank me for clearing your name. It was quite a sacrifice, as I'm sure you've learned. Two of my men died for the honor."

Fury blasted through her. "What a waste." She held his stare. "I'm certain I would have been exonerated in any event. I'm touched that you felt compelled to intervene on my behalf, but I can assure you it was a waste of your resources."

Rage flickered in his eyes before he schooled the reaction. "You are a fighter, Marissa Frasier. I've decided that forty-eight hours is far too much time. I will have your answer to my proposition today. Will you accept my proposal?"

If she told him no, he might kill them where they stood. If she said yes…

"As you can imagine, I haven't really had time to consider your proposal. Once I'm resettled in my home, I'm sure I'll be able to think more clearly and focus on where I go from here."

He moved closer still. Next to her Lacon tensed.

"Is there something or someone keeping you from making the right choice, Issy?"

His use of her nickname made her stomach churn. "I make my own decisions, Vito. I thought you would know that by now. Didn't William tell you how stubborn I can be?"

"I will have your answer," he pressed.

Lacon put a hand to the man's chest. "I'm beginning to think you suffer from selective hearing, *Vito*. She said she doesn't have an answer for you."

The other men in the room instantly drew their weapons and aimed them at Lacon. Marissa touched his arm. "It's all right. I think Vito understands."

The glare-off between Lacon and Anastasia lasted another ten disturbing seconds.

Anastasia stepped back from Lacon's firm hand. "You, Mr. Traynor, are pushing your luck."

Lacon dropped his arm to his side and laughed. "I've been pushing my luck my whole life, Anastasia. I don't think you're going to have anything at all to do with changing that. You see, Dr. Frasier is my responsibility. I listen only to her. Until she tells me to back off, I will be in your face. Got it?"

Five pulse-pounding seconds passed before the other man spoke. He turned his attention to Marissa. "I'll expect your answer before midnight. Do not disappoint me, Issy. You won't like my reaction."

Anastasia turned and walked out. The two men backed out behind him, weapons still trained on Lacon.

When the door closed, he moved lightning fast across the room and locked it. He stepped to the window and checked beyond the shade.

Marissa struggled to remain standing when her knees threatened to give out.

"They're gone."

Lacon turned and started walking toward her. Somehow she couldn't bring herself to move from this spot.

"He isn't going to let me go."

LACON WISHED HE could promise her that Anastasia would eventually move on, turn his attention elsewhere, but he knew that was not true. He'd done more research. The man was like a dog with a bone.

Once he set his sights on something, he wouldn't let go until it belonged to him.

"Let's take a break while I update Michaels. Maybe he'll have some news for us."

"You go ahead. I need to stay busy." She rubbed her hands up and down her arms as if she were cold.

He touched her cheek and offered the most reassuring smile he could. "I'll only be a minute."

She nodded and returned to the cleanup work. They'd finished upstairs. She pulled on her gloves and started scrubbing the bookshelves in her living room. Lacon put through the call and brought Michaels up to speed. He and Victoria had spoken, and her concern was that Anastasia would simply take what he wanted and kill anyone who got in his way. This was his MO, Michaels reminded him. Lacon had come to the same conclusion.

With a warning to get back to the safe house as soon as possible and to be careful, the call ended.

The sooner he helped Issy get through the work down here, the sooner he could coax her into going back to the safe house. She had mentioned staying here, but that was a no-go. She wouldn't like it, but he was confident he could convince her to listen to reason.

By the time the last of the fingerprint dust was cleaned up downstairs, the delivery truck had arrived with her new mattress and taken the old one away. Issy had lit her favorite scented candles to chase away the lingering odor of death. She'd opened a bottle of wine but Lacon had passed on the offer. His instincts were humming. Whatever Anastasia had planned when he didn't hear from her or didn't get the answer he wanted, Lacon wanted to be well prepared.

He tucked in his side of the clean sheet. "I don't think I've ever seen so many books outside a library," he teased.

She smiled, the first since that idiot's visit. "I've always loved reading. Growing up, we spent more time with books than with the television. I've never been able to give one away, so I keep them."

He reached for one of the new pillows and tucked it into place on his side of the bed. "I think you might need to consider a bigger house, maybe with a room to serve as a library."

"I thought about turning the third floor into one but I kind of like having a guest room when my brother visits. How about you, are you a book guy?"

They finished making the bed. "To tell you the truth, I haven't read a book since college. Never enough time."

"What now?" She glanced around the room as if searching for one more chore to do.

"We should head back to the safe house. I can protect you better there."

"What do I do about Anastasia? If I ignore his demand, he'll just come after us."

"We'll figure it out as we go." Lacon smiled, lifted her chin with his knuckle. "I do not want you over-analyzing this. We will figure it out."

She drew away from his touch. "You're probably right. I should pack a few things before we go."

He watched her walk toward the closet, worry nagging at him. He'd said or done something to upset her. When he felt more comfortable about her safety, he would make right whatever he'd done wrong.

Chapter Twelve

7:45 p.m.

“You’ve got everything?” Lacon picked up the bag she had packed.

Issy stood in the center of her living room looking lost. She had been more quiet than usual the past couple of hours. They’d finished the cleanup and set her home to rights. Every hour that passed seemed to make her draw more into herself. He wanted to ask if he’d said or done something, but the situation was getting far too intense for him to go there now. Keeping his head on straight was crucial.

She finally nodded. “I guess so.”

He, on the other hand, was already worried about how he would protect her when she returned to work tomorrow. By morning, Anastasia would be searching the city for her. He would be pissed as hell. No doubt he would come here and also go to the ER where she worked. The bastard would not stop until he found her.

Déjà vu was messing with Lacon's head. Flashes of memory from his attempts to protect Sherry had his gut in knots. *You're older and wiser now.* He hoped like hell the wisdom he had gained over the years would keep him smart and prepared for what he could feel coming.

"You're ready then?"

"I suppose." Issy glanced around one more time before walking toward him. "I'm ready if you are."

"I'll have a look around outside and check the car, then we're off."

"And I'll stay right here until you give me the all clear," she said, repeating his usual order.

They'd been over the way things would go from here. With Anastasia's edict, every move they made out in the open was riskier. He was growing more impatient. And that impatience made him all the more dangerous.

"You got it." Lacon reached for the door.

"You'll let your backup know?"

He gave her a nod. "Always do." He reached for the door once more.

"Wait."

He turned back to her as she pulled her cell phone from her pocket. She stared at the screen. "It's Anastasia."

His heart bumping into a faster rhythm, Lacon nodded. “Answer it.”

She took a breath, touched the screen. “Marissa Frasier.”

“I need you to make a house call, *Issy*.”

Her gaze collided with Lacon’s. He gave her a nod to continue.

“What kind of house call?”

“Based on your previous house calls, you can well imagine. My people work in the most dangerous parts of the city. The reception is not always a positive one. However, this particular one, I’m sure you can handle quickly.”

“What’s the address?”

He provided a South Calumet address, thirty-five minutes away on the other side of the river. Lacon instinctively calculated the most direct route.

“I’ll go now,” she said, her tone weary.

“When you’re finished, Issy,” Anastasia said, “I need your answer.”

The call ended.

Her gaze moved up to Lacon’s, worry clouding her green eyes. “We have to go, I know.” She shook her head, tears welling in her eyes. “But I don’t want to. I don’t want to be his puppet again.”

For the first time in his career, he second-guessed the decisions he’d made about the case so far. “We could just leave. Get in the car and keep driving.”

She smiled sadly. “We could.”

For a couple of seconds the possibility crackled between them with such promise. But they both knew running wasn't the answer.

He laughed. "But then we'd just have to be back by tomorrow so you could make your shift at the Edge."

Her smile lightened the tiniest bit. "True." She sighed. "I guess we should just do this thing."

He nodded. "Guess so." He reached for the door once more. "I'll have that look around first—just in case—and then we'll go."

"I'll be waiting for your signal."

His right hand on the grip of his weapon, he moved out the door and down the steps. Sidewalk was clear. No passengers in any of the parked vehicles as far as he could see. He walked to the car, popped the trunk and dropped her bag inside. He sent Michaels a text with the address of where they were headed, then surveyed the street again as he closed the lid.

He sensed the man behind him before the bastard made a sound.

"Get your hands out where I can see them."

Son of a bitch.

When he didn't obey the command quickly enough, a muzzle bored into the back of his skull.

"Take it easy." Lacon held his hands out on either side of him.

A hand patted his jacket then reached beneath for his weapon. "Let's go back in the house now."

For an instant he considered trying to tackle the guy. There was always the chance the first shot would miss. The trouble was, there were likely two of them, and if he did anything stupid and got himself killed, Issy would be completely at their mercy.

So he did as he was told.

They climbed the steps and walked through the door.

Lacon had cleared the door when Issy screamed.

He pivoted.

The thug's weapon discharged.

Lacon's brain assimilated a number of things simultaneously. Issy had hit the man's arm with something that looked like a fireplace poker. The man with the gun howled in agony. The weapon he'd dropped spun across the floor.

Lacon made a dive for the weapon. He hoped like hell a neighbor would call the cops about the gunfire.

"Leave the weapon or I will shoot her."

Lacon didn't immediately remove his hand from the gun on the floor. He shifted his attention to the new man in the room, the one holding the muzzle of his weapon against Issy's temple. The first guy had snatched the poker from her and stood glaring at her as if he wanted to deliver a little payback.

Damn it all to hell. Lacon pushed to his feet, hands in the air. "You probably should call your boss. He wants Dr. Frasier to take care of a situation over on South Calumet."

The two men exchanged a look, and then the one

with the gun on Issy laughed. "That was for your backup. He'll be rushing over to South Calumet, but not the two of you. Now, let's go."

The guy with the poker strode toward Lacon, nudged him with it. "Back off."

When Lacon had taken a couple of steps back, the bastard reclaimed his weapon and tossed the poker aside. "Anybody else does something stupid, and I'm putting a bullet in *your* head." He pointed to Lacon. "You got that?" he growled at Issy.

She glowered at him. "Got it."

The younger thug took Issy out the back door first. The older guy trailed Lacon, nudging him regularly with the muzzle of his weapon. They walked down the narrow driveway Lacon had opted not to use for parking when they arrived today to avoid the possibility of his car being trapped in the event of a takeover exactly like this one.

So much for trying to cover all the bases.

Once they reached the street that ran behind Issy's home, they made a right and walked half a block to a black sedan.

"You." The man behind him jabbed Lacon in the ribs with his weapon. "Get in the front passenger seat."

The other guy forced Issy into the back and slid in beside her.

When they were all in the car, the guy in the

back warned, "Keep in mind, Traynor, you make one wrong move, she gets it."

"Give me your cell phones," the driver demanded.

Lacon handed over his phone. The guy tossed it out the window.

"Let's have it," the guy in the back snapped at Issy.

A couple seconds later his window went down, and Issy's phone hit the ground.

Lacon should never have allowed her to leave the safe house. He shouldn't have allowed her to go along with the police in hopes of trapping Anastasia.

The problem was, none of those choices had been his. Issy had wanted to take Anastasia down. She had known that he would never stop coming after her as long as he was out there and still drawing breath.

Lacon had every intention of changing one or both of those things.

North Burling Street

IT WAS DARK by the time they pulled through the gate onto Anastasia's compound. Marissa imagined they had waited for the cover of dark to approach his home. They'd driven around far longer than necessary to come straight here from her place by any reasonable route.

The thug who'd dragged her out of the car and was now gripping her arm ushered her across the expansive yard. He was still favoring his right arm, which she supposed was why he held on to her with his left hand. She wished she had hit him harder and on the head. If she'd moved faster, maybe Lacon would have been able to grab his weapon before the other man could stop him.

She glanced around, wishing there was a full moon tonight. The landscape lighting she had noticed on her and Lacon's previous visit was missing tonight. The sound of the water in the reflecting pond dribbled in the darkness, adding another layer of eeriness to the fear expanding inside her. Her heart beat faster and faster as they neared the rear of the house. She glanced over her shoulder twice, making sure Lacon and the other thug were still behind them.

She was going to get him killed. William's stupidity and her plummet into that same stupidity were going to cost this man his life. She had to do something. He was doing his job, yes. He was aware of the danger, yes. But the potential end result wasn't right any way she looked at it. She could not allow this to happen.

Once through the French doors, the thugs ushered the two of them away from the main living area and down a long hall. Finally, they crowded into what appeared to be a storage room. Shelves loaded with dry goods and household supplies lined the walls. The bastard clutching her arm reached for a box of detergent, but when he moved it a portion of the shelving slid away, revealing a staircase.

Just like in a bad movie. How would Lacon's backup, Ian Michaels, or the police find them here?

At the bottom of the stairs was a fair-sized room that looked somewhat like a small den. The typical U-shaped sectional sofa was arranged atop thick beige carpet. Rich paneled walls gave the basement room a more classic look. A large television and a fireplace sat on opposite ends of the space. On each of the other two walls was a door. One might have gone to a bathroom and the other maybe to a bedroom. Except the one on the farthest wall from where they now stood had a keypad and looked more like a panic room door. That was the direction in which they headed, and dread swelled like a rock inside her stomach.

"Where is Vito?" She jerked at the man's hold. "I need to speak with him."

"In due time," the thug said. The keypad had the usual numbers for entering a code, but it also had a biometric pad. The man pressed his thumb there and the door swung inward.

He pushed Marissa inside. Digging in her heels, she didn't make it easy.

Lacon was shoved in right behind her.

"Make yourselves at home," the thug who'd dragged her here said. "For now." He laughed until the door closed, blocking the awful sound and any possibility of escape.

"You okay?" Lacon touched her arm.

She stared at the angry red marks the man's grip had created. "He didn't hurt me. Just made me mad as hell."

He pulled her into his arms and hugged her. "Don't try to be a hero, Issy. Just do what they ask until help comes."

She drew back and stared up at him, searching his pale brown eyes. With every fiber of her being, she had feared this moment would come. "How do you know they'll be able to find us?"

He smiled. "It's the Colby Agency. They always do."

She couldn't do this. She should never have involved anyone else. Somehow she had to rectify that mistake.

"Lacon, I appreciate how well you've taken care of me the past few days." She drew out of his embrace and squared her shoulders, hanging on to the last threads of her courage. "But I don't want you to do anything else. I want you to just stop. Right now."

"What?" The word came out on a choked laugh. "Are you firing me again?"

"Yes. I'm firing you as my bodyguard." She folded her arms over her chest in hopes he wouldn't notice the way her body had started to tremble. "You…" She cleared the emotion from her throat. "You are not to take any additional measures to defend me in any way. From this moment, your only concern is staying alive."

For ten or so seconds he stared at her as if he

were too stunned to speak. To escape his daunting stare, she allowed herself to look around the room and fully assess the situation for the first time. It was far larger than the room outside that door. No warm paneling or soft carpet. Just cold concrete walls and floors. There were only two chairs, and each had straps to secure a person's arms and legs. Her body trembled harder when she considered the steel table, much like the one found in an operating room, complete with straps for securing whoever might end up stretched out on it.

Nearby, a glass-front cabinet displayed drug vials, very similar to those found in the dispensary at the Edge, along its top shelf. The other shelves were filled with what could only be called the tools of torture. Scalpels, knives, a hammer, small forceps, a hacksaw and a multitude of others she couldn't fully see.

She had to look away. It didn't help. Her gaze next landed on a heavy chain that hung from the ceiling. The hook on the end suggested it was for hanging something or…*someone*. Another small table, this one with wheels, sat close by. A control box of some sort with various attached cables sat atop it. She could only imagine what it was.

"Did you have anything else you wanted to say?" Lacon stared at her, his hands resting on his lean hips.

Emotion tangled in her throat. "No." She cleared her throat. "I guess that's all I have to say."

He laughed as he, too, took stock of their situation. "Well, you picked a hell of a time to decide to fire me."

A tear escaped her fierce hold, and she swiped at the nuisance. "Sorry. I don't have a lot of experience with this sort of thing."

He grabbed her and pulled her against him. "You can't fire me, Issy," he said, his tone as desperate as the look in his eyes. "This stopped being about work the first time I kissed you."

Those damned tears spilled past her lashes in spite of all she did to attempt to staunch them. "I do not want you to risk your life for me. Just do whatever they tell you until…until we get out of here. All I need is your word that you'll do as I say."

He smiled and her heart reacted. "I can't promise you that, Issy. We're in this together, and I'm not backing down. I'll do whatever I have to do to keep you safe. That's what people who care about each other do, so don't ask me to do otherwise."

She exhaled a frustrated breath. "Fine. Just don't take any unnecessary risks."

He grunted a sound that couldn't be called an agreement. Before she could argue her point further, he took her by the hand and ushered her along to the cabinet near the steel table. He checked the doors. Locked. She doubted he had expected otherwise.

"Stand back," he ordered.

She moved a few feet away as he turned his back

to the cabinet and then elbowed one of the glass doors. The glass shattered. He reached inside and grabbed a knife and the hammer. What in the world would he be able to do with those?

The glass crackled under his boots as he walked back to where she waited. He offered her the hammer. "You have a pretty mean swing, so here you go. A weapon."

Her trembling lips slid into a smile despite the fear and worry spiraling madly inside her. "My brother liked to play cops and robbers when we were kids. Conking him over the head was my favorite part. No matter how many times we played that game, he never resisted, even when he knew that bop on the head was coming."

Grinning, Lacon slid the knife into his waistband. "I think I like your brother." He hugged her again. This time he pressed his lips close to her ear and whispered, "There are cameras. They'll take these weapons away from us when they come back." He drew back a little and kissed her hard on the mouth, his right hand sliding down her back, fingers slipping into her hip pockets. He pulled his mouth from hers and hugged her again and murmured, "I'm hoping they won't find the scalpel I just slid into your back pocket on the right."

The door opened and they drew apart. Lacon grabbed her hand and ushered her behind him. Marissa wished she could think of something to say or do that would somehow change what she feared would happen next.

"Put the weapons down!" the thug she'd whacked with the poker shouted, his weapon trained on Lacon.

The thug's friend waltzed in next, his weapon leveled on Marissa. "Come with me," he ordered.

She shook her head. "Only if he goes, too."

"No can do." He motioned with his weapon for her to come with him. "The boss only wants you."

Fear blasted through her veins. "If you want me, you'll have to come and get me." She gripped the hammer a little tighter.

The one with his weapon aimed at Lacon was taller and older, and he walked closer. "Do as he says or I'll shoot your boyfriend."

Fear exploded in her chest. What the hell did she do now? She divided her attention between the two men coming closer.

"Put the hammer down," Lacon said, "and do like he said."

She swung her gaze to him. "No."

He sent her a desperate but determined look. "You go with him. Don't worry, I'll catch up."

The younger thug grabbed her. She swung the hammer at his head, missed. Tried again to hit him before her pathetic weapon flew from her grasp. His arm went around her waist, and the barrel of his weapon nudged into her temple.

"You behave yourself, Doc, and I won't have to hurt you. Mr. Anastasia wouldn't be too happy about that."

Her eyes stayed on Lacon until the bastard dragged her out the door. She wanted to kill him. She wanted to scream. To cry.

Mostly she wanted to kill Vito Anastasia.

The man hauled her up the stairs and into the long hall that led back into the main living area of the house. She relaxed a little and didn't fight him as much. So far he hadn't checked for any other weapons. *Please don't let him look.*

He stopped at a door before they reached the grand entry hall. She wondered where the fancy butler and the kitchen staff were this evening. Did they all blindly go about their business while their boss did horrific things to their guests? The urge to scream burgeoned in her throat. The need surged with such intensity, it was all she could do to hold back the sound. But she didn't want to do anything that would make this thug angry. The one thing she had on her side was that scalpel.

Maybe that narrow piece of steel would be the miracle she needed.

The thug pushed the door open. The room was empty save a couple of wooden chairs and a video monitor mounted to the white walls. The floor, ceiling and walls were so white they were blinding.

"Sit," the thug ordered.

He pushed her toward one of the chairs, and she

hit the floor in front of it on her hands and knees. She ignored the pain in her wrists and knees and climbed into the chair.

"Are you going to behave yourself or do I need to tie you to the damned chair?"

She glared up at him but didn't say a word. "What could I possibly do?"

"Good." He laughed. "I'll be back." He hesitated at the door and pointed to a place in the ceiling where the flow of white ballooned out like a basketball. "That's a camera. We'll be watching every move you make."

There had to be something she could do to stop this. "I want to see Vito. He will not be happy that you're treating me this way."

The man sneered at her. "He knows you're here. You'll see him soon enough. Just relax and enjoy the show."

She frowned. Show? What show?

The monitor on the wall flickered and then the image cleared. The scene on the screen was from the basement. Lacon and the older thug were still facing off—the thug's gun aimed at Lacon… Lacon still holding the knife.

"Oh my God." She stood, moved closer to the monitor.

There was no sound, so she couldn't hear what they were saying. The man with the gun gestured to the steel table. Lacon placed the knife there and backed away. The thug picked it up and pitched it aside. Then he gestured to the table again. This time Lacon hopped onto the table's edge and then lay down.

"No." Her hand went to her mouth.

The man made another motion with the gun and said something else she couldn't hear.

Lacon fastened the first of the straps, securing himself to the table.

Marissa touched the screen and began to scream.

Chapter Thirteen

The door opened and Marissa's personal thug charged into the room. "What the hell is wrong with you?" he demanded.

She pointed at the monitor. "If your friend hurts my friend, then I'm done here. My answer to Anastasia's proposal will be no."

The bastard laughed. "Don't you get it yet, Doc? No isn't an option."

The door behind him was open. If she could only get past him and to a phone. She turned back to the monitor and started to scream again.

He stormed across the expanse of tile that lay between them and reached up to turn off the monitor. That's when she bolted.

She ran for the entry hall. The front door was right there. With the house so close to the street, all she had to do was get outside and scream at the top of her lungs. Someone would surely hear her. All she needed was one person to call the police and report the disturbance. The Colby Agency would be looking for them already.

Afraid to slow down as she reached the entry hall, she slammed against the door and twisted the lock. Her fingers curled around the door handle. Her heart swelled. Get out the door and—

"Open that door and your friend dies."

Her fingers stilled on the handle. Her heart thundered; her blood roared in her ears. But he was right…if she did this, they would kill Lacon. He probably had a gun pointed at her head even as he spoke. She had banked on the idea that he wouldn't shoot her for fear of Anastasia's wrath.

She dropped her hands to her sides and turned to face him. "I want to see Vito."

As if he'd been waiting just around the corner listening, Anastasia stepped into view. "Do we have a problem, Issy?"

"We need to talk." She steadied herself, met his gaze with defiance in her own. "Privately."

He smiled. "At last."

With a wave of his hand he dismissed the thug, then he gestured for her to come to him. Forcing one foot in front of the other, she moved closer and closer to the monster who would forevermore play the lead in all her nightmares—assuming she lived through this night.

With a hand at the small of her back, he ushered her toward the grand staircase.

"We'll have more privacy upstairs."

Doing all within her power to prevent her body from shaking with the new fear spreading through her, she ascended the stairs at his side. She needed him to believe she wanted to cooperate. If she could somehow barter Lacon's release, she might have to bide her time until he and the Colby Agency figured out the best way to rescue her.

As much as the idea sickened her, she would do whatever was necessary until then.

"Did the situation on South Calumet work itself out?" she asked. Her voice was a little thinner than she would have liked, but at least it wasn't shaking.

He smiled at her. Her stomach cramped with disgust. "It did. Thank you for asking."

Upstairs, the house was as elegantly decorated as downstairs. How was it such a vicious man could have such opulent taste?

The spacious corridor went left and right. He directed her to the right. At the end of the corridor stood double doors. Renewed terror licked a path up her spine. His private rooms, which probably included a bedroom.

Stay cool. You can do this. All she needed was one minute with a phone to call for help. Then maybe both she and Lacon would be rescued.

He opened the doors to a sitting room. More double doors that stood beyond the sofa likely led to his more private rooms. The windows on either side of the generous space offered magnificent views, as well as another opportunity for her. A small occasional chair sat next to the sofa. She could probably pick it up and hurl it toward the window. If she succeeded in breaking the glass, the alarm would likely go off.

Pay attention, Issy. Find the right opportunity.

"Please." He gestured to the sofa. "Make yourself comfortable and I'll open the champagne. This is reason to celebrate."

She sat down, felt the slim steel in her pocket that didn't give with the move. The scalpel's presence gave her comfort. *Thank you, Lacon.* "I'd like to discuss the terms of our arrangement, but first I have one condition."

The cork popped. "You're a brilliant woman, Issy. I expected you would have certain conditions."

Hearing the sizzle of the bubbly drink overflowing was when she realized that he'd had a bottle of champagne chilling in a silver bucket of ice. Two stemmed glasses sat on the table next to the bucket. He'd prepared for this moment. Asking her to give him an answer had only been another of his games. He had always planned to have his wish, one way or another. The possibility that nothing she said or did would impact how this turned out made her start to shake deep inside.

No. This was the twenty-first century. People didn't get to enslave other people in this country…

unless they didn't get caught. Panic burgeoned inside her. She thought of the high-profile victims she'd read about in the news who had been held for years—decades—by men with far fewer resources than Vito Anastasia.

Focus, Issy. No losing hope.

While he poured the bubbly liquid, she collected herself. By the time he joined her at the sofa, she had decided to go with the strategy she'd already begun in her head. She accepted the glass he offered and announced, "This first condition is nonnegotiable."

He savored the drink. "I'm quite curious as to what that condition is."

"Let him go. You let him go and my answer is yes—assuming we agree on a couple of other terms."

He smiled. "By him, you mean your friend—your bodyguard who held you and kissed you like a lover."

She shrugged. "Being a physician is a demanding job. You get lonely. Sometimes a woman as busy as I am needs someone, even if I am paying him for other services. Handy is sometimes the only option." She prayed he didn't see the lie in her words.

He nodded. "I understand. My position is much the same. Loneliness goes with the territory." He draped his arm over the back of the sofa and touched her hair. "But neither of us has to be alone again."

As difficult as it proved, she forced a smile, resisting the need to shudder. "Then you agree to my first condition."

"I will consider it." He finished his glass and set it on the cocktail table. "But I fear there may be a glitch in doing so."

She frowned. "What glitch?"

"I pride myself in my ability to measure a man. This man will not willingly ride off into the sunset, leaving you behind."

"He will do exactly what I tell him to do." If her heart pounded any harder, she was sure he would see it threatening to burst from her chest.

"He'll only bring the authorities and others from his agency, and I fear if that happens you might not stand by our agreement."

"You have my word." She sipped her drink. "Now, if that's settled, let's move on. I'll need to give the Edge a two-week notice. Otherwise my reputation will be damaged, and I've worked too hard to allow that to happen." Another sip for her dry throat. "I'm going to want four times my current salary. I'm sure that's far more than you paid William but I'm a far better physician than he was, and smarter."

One side of his mouth lifted in a smile. "Your excitement sounds quite convincing, Issy. What changed your mind?"

Keep him talking. Keep him off guard. Lacon's backup would be calling his boss and the police by now. Help would come.

"Oh I'm not finished yet." She placed her glass on the table. "I will not live in that carriage house. Too cramped, too confining. I noticed a very nice town house across the street. It's not for sale, but I'm certain you can take care of that."

He studied her, appeared to be amused. "Either you've considered the situation at length, or you're playing me to buy time." The amusement vanished. "Which is it, Issy?"

"You're right. I've spent a great deal of time pondering my dilemma. Since I don't want to end up like William, and the police don't seem capable of stopping you, why fight the inevitable? I've always considered myself quite pragmatic in matters related to my career and my financial future."

His narrowed gaze relaxed. "Assuming I meet your first condition and your other terms."

"Assuming so, yes."

He stood. Her heart stumbled. She pushed to her feet and followed him to the windows that overlooked the back of his property. *Think!* Whatever was happening to Lacon, she had to stop it now.

"If your people harm him, I'm afraid our negotiations will be over."

Anastasia shifted his attention to her once more. "You present quite the quandary, Issy."

"It's really quite simple. You let him go—I stay."

He reached out, touched the pulse at the base of her throat. "You want me to believe you're calm and confident, that your decision is made. But I can feel your terror, Issy. How am I supposed to trust your words when your body tells me a completely different story?"

"You want me here with you, isn't that right?" She moved nearer to him. "Not just my ability as a physician, but *me*." She held her breath, touched his face, traced the line of his jaw. He stood stone still, but his eyes gave her the answer she sought. She was right. "I'm here and I'm willing to stay."

He smiled, the expression tight, angry. "Do you believe me a fool?"

She fought to keep the trembling at bay. "Why would I think that?"

"I saw the way he kissed you. The way you responded. You will sacrifice yourself for him, and then you will run the first opportunity that presents itself."

She set her hands on her hips. "You had me brought here like a prisoner. I've offered you a deal and you don't seem interested. Why don't you take me back home, and when you make up *your* mind, you can call me."

Every ounce of courage she possessed was required to turn her back on him and to start walking toward the door.

If he had a weapon, he could draw it right now and shoot her. It was a risk she had to take. Lacon could be dying at this very moment. She had to help him.

A ruthless grip curled around her left arm. "No one walks away from me." He yanked her around to face him. "You will do exactly as I say, or everyone you care about will die, starting with your friend downstairs."

Stay strong. Don't let him see more than he already has.

"I offered to do exactly as you say. I gave you my terms."

"This is not a negotiation, as you appear to believe." His grip tightened on her arm. "You are now my property. There are no other terms or conditions. I've warned you of the consequences if you refuse to cooperate."

"You're right. I don't know what I was thinking." She hooked the thumb of her free hand in her right pocket. "I will do whatever you say. Just let my friend go and I'm good."

His evil smile was back. "I'm afraid it's too late for your friend. You see, Raeford fancies himself a coroner. He often practices on those we find in our way."

"You asshole," she snarled.

He threw his head back and laughed. "You should see your face."

While he continued to laugh, her fingers dipped into her back pocket, wrapped around the handle of the scalpel.

"I hope you're wrong, Vito," she warned.

He shook his head and laughed some more. "Oh, I'm not wrong, Issy. I'm never wrong."

"Too bad."

She stepped toward him and stabbed the scalpel into his throat.

He twisted. The cold steel sank into him.

He howled and reached for the scalpel. Blood seeped between his fingers.

She ran.

He had moved, so she missed the artery she had been aiming for. If she was really, really lucky, maybe she'd landed a fatal wound anyway. There were several veins and arteries in the neck.

A gunshot exploded in the air. The bullet hit the doorframe as she rushed from the room.

She ran faster, hoping the pain and any bleeding would slow him down.

Stairs.

She hit the stairs running. Two at a time. She almost fell. Grabbed the railing to catch herself and kept going.

Another shot.

The bullet pinged on the metal railing right behind her.

He was still coming.

Oh God.

TOP THUG TIGHTENED the strap on Lacon's right wrist. "I apologize for the delay, Mr. Traynor. Sometimes my associate feels he doesn't ever get to be in on the real fun stuff." He moved on to the end of the table and reached for the first of the two straps there.

"These younger guys, they think they're owed something for doing nothing more than breathing." He laughed. "But he'll learn, or who knows, maybe I'll lose my patience and blow his head off."

The two men had almost come to punches arguing about who would have the pleasure of torturing Lacon and who would coordinate the security team outside. Both men were fully aware that the Colby Agency would send backup when it became apparent their client and investigator were missing in action.

The good news was that the argument had given Lacon the opportunity to unfasten the strap on his left hand since the disagreement had broken out before his right was restrained. He'd quickly arranged the strap so that it still looked fastened.

Top Thug returned to Lacon's side. "Now we're ready to begin."

"Where's Dr. Frasier?" He had asked that question three times already, mostly just to make the man hesitate.

"She's conferring with Mr. Anastasia." He grinned. "I imagine he's learning all her secrets by now."

Fury stormed through Lacon. He gritted his teeth and stayed perfectly still while the older man opened the cabinet. More broken glass scattered on the floor.

"This should do nicely." He turned back to the table, the other scalpel Lacon had noticed among the tools in his hand. "I'm so intrigued by the inner workings of the human body. I should have become a surgeon."

"I'll bet Dr. Frasier could give you a few pointers."

He laughed again. "I doubt she'll be very happy with me when she learns what I've done to you. You won't care one way or another because you'll be dead." He placed the scalpel on the table between Lacon's legs. "Let's start with the chest. So much to work with there. I almost always start with the torso."

One by one he released the buttons of Lacon's shirt. He pushed back the sides to expose his chest. "Here we go." He reached for the scalpel.

Lacon made his move. He socked the older man in the face, sending him tumbling backward and falling into the cabinet. Lacon shook his hand, ignoring the pain from the impact that had no doubt broken the old bastard's nose. He unfastened the strap on his right hand and the one around his waist. He had his right foot free before the man staggered back to the table, blood pouring down his face.

"You son of a bitch." Top Thug drew his weapon.

Lacon kicked his wrist, sending the weapon flying. A second kick hit him in the chest. Top Thug slammed to the floor this time.

Lacon released his left foot and jumped off the table. He snagged the gun before the bastard could reach it. "On the table! Now!"

Top Thug started to argue, but Lacon shoved the gun in his face. "On the table."

The older man scooted onto the table. Lacon quickly strapped him in and felt in his pockets for his cell phone. “What’s the code for the door?”

The man laughed. “Don’t you wish you knew?”

The keypad also had a biometric thumb print scanner. “No problem.” Lacon rounded the table and snagged the hacksaw from the cabinet. “Which hand do you want to keep?”

He shouted the code.

“Where did Anastasia take her?”

“To his suite. Upstairs.”

Lacon rushed from the room and raced up the stairs to the first floor. He cracked the door open and listened before stepping out into the deserted hall.

The sound of a gunshot in the main living area had him bursting into the corridor.

He eased in that direction, listening for more trouble.

A scream.

Issy.

He charged forward, ran headlong into the younger thug who’d brought them here. He whipped the barrel of his weapon toward Lacon, but he didn’t fire quickly enough—the bullet from Lacon’s weapon nailed him center chest. The thug dropped like a rock. Lacon grabbed the downed man’s weapon and shoved it into the waistband of his jeans.

He made it as far as the entry hall without encountering anyone else. There, the front door abruptly opened. A man dressed all in black, including a face mask, stepped inside. Perimeter security. Lacon fired in his direction. He scrambled back out the door.

Another scream.

Lacon shifted toward the staircase.

Anastasia was dragging Issy up the steps.

Lacon rushed for the stairs. The front door opened again. This time he didn't fire wide of his target. He popped the guy in the shoulder. He disappeared outside the door again.

Lacon took the stairs three at a time. He was at the top before the man in black made another attempt to come inside.

Shouting sounded somewhere in the vicinity of the back of the downstairs area. Kitchen or den. More of Anastasia's men were coming. Damn it. They were running out of time.

The double doors at the end of the hall closed as Lacon headed down that corridor. Lacon sent Michaels an SOS text and the address in case he hadn't already narrowed down where they might be.

He shoved the phone into his pocket and moved slowly toward the double doors, listening for the slightest sound from the room.

Voices. Heated words. They were arguing.

Lacon stood to one side and turned the knob. He opened the door a narrow crack and peeked beyond it.

Anastasia had Issy by the hair, the muzzle of his weapon shoved against her throat. Blood oozed from a wound in his neck. The scalpel, Lacon decided. *Good girl, Issy.*

"Join us, won't you, Mr. Traynor."

Lacon cleared his mind and focused on one thing: stopping this bastard. He stepped in the room, then to his right, putting his back to the wall so none of Anastasia's men could sneak up on him. There was blood on her T-shirt. Fear ignited in his veins. "You okay, Issy?"

"Yes."

She didn't sound okay.

"Let her go," he offered, "and you and I will finish this. The winner takes all."

Anastasia laughed. "This," he glared at Lacon, "is my world. You don't get to set the rules, Mr. Traynor. You're both going to die."

"If that's your final decision," Lacon said, "I can live with that."

Anastasia swung his weapon, aiming it toward Lacon. "I just told you that you're going to die."

Lacon didn't bother responding. He put a bullet in the guy's head.

The weapon fell from his hand and he crumpled to the floor.

Issy rushed to him. "Are you hurt?" She looked him up and down.

"You're the one with blood all over you."

She threw her arms around him and hugged him hard. "They were going to kill you."

"We're not in the clear yet," he warned.

He'd no more said the words than the sound of running footfalls echoed from the corridor.

He jerked his head toward the nearest door. Issy didn't look happy, but she disappeared behind it.

Lacon moved into a firing stance facing the double doors and held his breath to calm the blood roaring in his ears. A man in black rushed into the room, his weapon drawn. He spotted his boss and as if he'd sensed Lacon's presence he whirled toward him.

"You could leave now," Lacon offered, "and live."

"But then I'd miss the fun of watching your brains splatter on the wall."

The door behind which Issy had disappeared suddenly opened. The other man glanced in that direction. Lacon took the shot.

The man dropped.

But there was at least one more in the corridor.

Lacon braced for his arrival.

The sound of footsteps disappearing in the opposite direction made him smile. The other guy was retreating.

"Chicago PD! Drop your weapon!"

The proclamation echoed from somewhere downstairs.

The cavalry was here.

Issy stepped from her hiding place and looked

from him to the man on the floor. “Did I hear the police?”

Lacon nodded. “Thanks.” When her gaze met his in question, he went on. “You probably saved my life when you opened that door.”

She shrugged. “I could hear what was happening and I didn’t know what else to do to distract him.”

More footfalls thundered up the stairs. Lacon placed his weapon in his waistband and held his hands up.

SWAT poured into the room. By the time they had determined that Lacon and Issy were the good guys, Michaels, Nader and Watts were walking through the door.

It was over. He glanced at Issy as she answered Nader’s questions.

And they were both still alive.

Chapter Fourteen

Hampden Court, Saturday, July 14, 6:55 p.m.

The doorbell chimed its tune through the house.

Marissa's nerves jangled. She checked her reflection in the full-length mirror once more. She had pinned her wild curls up in a makeshift French twist with a few spiral wisps clinging to her temple and her neck. Good as it gets, she decided. Now for a little mascara, a touch of peppermint-flavored, shiny lip gloss and she was ready.

She drew in a deep breath for courage. The black dress hit four inches above her knees, not too modest yet not overly brazen. Sleeveless, scooped neck but not too revealing. The fit of the soft fabric made her feel sexy. The dress hugged her curves, adding a distinct sense of femininity without going overboard.

Then there were the shoes. Decent three-inch heels in a classic open-toed pump.

The chime came again, making her pulse flutter.

No more dawdling.

Taking her time, mostly to ensure she didn't break her neck in the heels, she descended the stairs. She spent so much time in comfortable work shoes, strutting around in heels was not one of her better skills.

When she reached the door, she paused. Had she forgotten a dab of perfume? She thought for a moment before distinctly recalling picking up the cut-glass bottle.

"No need to be nervous, Issy," she murmured as she wrapped her fingers around the knob and gave it a twist. She smiled. "Hi."

There were a host of other things she'd intended to say, like "come in" and "nice to see you" and "oh what lovely flowers." The rest of the words deserted her as her hungry gaze drank in the gorgeous man standing at her door.

Lacon Traynor wore jeans, as usual, plus a cotton button-up in a soft blue that emphasized his tanned skin. And those well-loved cowboy boots. She noted the white daisies, purple roses and bright yellow sunflowers in his hand on her tour back up to his handsome face. His sandy blond hair was combed as if it was Sunday morning and he was ready to go to church. His golden eyes were watching her admire him, and she didn't mind at all. She did admire him, in so many ways.

"Hey." He smiled and her heart melted.

"Come in." She drew the door open wider, held on

for fear her knees would give out on her. She'd never met a man who could so easily make her swoon. In fact, she was fairly certain she'd never swooned before meeting Lacon Traynor.

He stepped inside and she closed the door. He offered her the flowers. "There's a flower stand in my neighborhood that swears all their flowers come fresh from a farm outside the city. I hope you like them."

She accepted the bouquet. "They're beautiful. Have a seat while I put these in water."

She took a couple of steps backward. "I'll only be a minute."

In the kitchen she rummaged under the sink for a pitcher, then placed it in the sink and filled it with water. Her hands shook as she loosened the ribbon around the arrangement. There was no need to be nervous. She knew this man. They had shared their bodies, laughed and cried and narrowly escaped death during a four-day period. Even in that short time, they had made memories that would forever be inscribed on the surface of her heart.

Wherever their fledgling relationship went from here, she couldn't be certain, but she had never in her life wanted to explore the possibilities with anyone more than she did with Lacon.

He walked up beside her, picked up a rose from the bundle and tucked it into the vase with the rest. "I made dinner reservations at your favorite restaurant."

Marissa picked up the vase. "You did?"

"Eva said Boka is your favorite."

She smiled. "Wow. I'm impressed you went to so much trouble."

He took the vase from her. Lifted his eyebrows in question.

"The table." She gestured to the dining room.

"No trouble." He placed the vase with its gorgeous arrangement on the table. "I wanted to take you someplace special."

They had talked about this. Or she had, rather. She'd spent her adult life immersed in school and then in her career. Eighty-hour weeks at work, the rest of her time spent at home sleeping or blindly walking through life with a man she never really knew. She had no idea if William had had a hobby, much less what restaurant was his favorite. They were always too busy. Their marriage had been nothing more than a mutually advantageous living arrangement with the occasional fringe benefit of handy sex. The latter had become as rare as a blue moon the final months they were together.

She never wanted that sort of relationship again. This go-around, she wanted complete intimacy. She wanted to share her entire life with her partner. She wanted to know him inside and out, and she wanted him to know her the same way. No secrets. No lies. Utter honesty and the sharing of all things, good, bad and otherwise.

No one was perfect, not her, not Lacon, and she wanted their relationship to embrace those imperfections.

If he wanted the same.

After all, four days was not even a week, which was why they had agreed to stay apart for two weeks. They had needed distance and time to know if this was real. Except they only made it just shy of twelve days.

The longest eleven plus days of her life.

He reached out, traced the line of her jaw. "I've missed you."

She smiled, his words sending desire singing through her veins. "I missed you, too."

His fingers slid down her arm, tugged her closer. "Is this where we start?"

"Do you still want to move forward?"

His arms went around her waist, pulled her snug against his body. "I have spent the past eleven days, ten hours and forty—" he checked his phone "—forty-four minutes thinking about nothing but you. I've relived every moment we spent together at least a hundred times. I go to sleep needing you and wake up still wanting you. My life before walking into this house and seeing you for the first time feels like someone else's. This is my life now...*you* are my life now."

When she stared, speechless, at him, he smiled. "Does that answer your question?"

He dipped his head, placed a tender kiss on her lips. "I want to take you all the places you dream of going. I want to make pretty babies with you." He nuzzled the sensitive skin under her ear. "I love you, Issy. I want to be the one who grows old with you."

She cupped his face in her hands and looked into his eyes. "I think maybe you should cancel that dinner reservation."

He followed her up the stairs as he made the call. She kicked her shoes off at the door to her room and waited, trembling with anticipation, while he unzipped her dress. He kissed each vertebra as he revealed it. By the time the dress slid down her body, she was burning up for him. He turned her around and surveyed the lacy black bra and skimpy panties in the same racy black lace.

"Oh man, I don't know how much of this I can take without losing it."

She laughed, the happiness filling her chest and erupting from her, making her heart glad. Together they released the buttons of his shirt, peeled it from his muscular body. She smoothed her palms over those gorgeous ridges and planes. He walked backward, his lips locked with hers until they reached the bed. She pushed him into a sitting position and reached for a boot.

The boots and socks landed near her shoes. He lay back and allowed her to dispense with his jeans, as well. She slid the well-fitting denim over his hips and down his muscular legs. Then she reached for the briefs, tugging them away from his thick, fully aroused penis.

Twelve days she had waited to have him inside her again. She straddled his body. He used his magic fingers to push aside the flimsy strap of silk between her thighs and to guide himself into her.

Her eyes closed as she slid fully down onto him. He growled with need. His hands slipped beneath the lacy cups and squeezed her breasts. She wanted to tell him how very much she had missed him… how desperately she had wanted to call him each and every damned night.

He watched her coming undone, and for a moment she paused and leaned down close enough to taste his lips. "I love you, Lacon Traynor. I can't imagine spending my life with anyone else. We will make pretty babies."

Feeling his body tremble beneath her, she sat up and ground herself into him, the urgency forcing her to start that frantic rhythm once more. She rode him faster and faster as the sweet throb of orgasm started deep inside, claiming her all too soon. Before she could catch her breath, he had rolled her onto her back and started the whole mind-blowing journey over again.

She didn't care if they ever left the house again. She had everything she wanted right here.

Chapter Fifteen

The Colby Agency, Monday, July 16, 9:30 a.m.

Victoria Colby-Camp sat behind her desk and smiled at Lucas as they waited for Jamie, their beloved granddaughter, to arrive.

"I worry that she's only nineteen," Victoria confessed. "Are we getting ahead of ourselves here?"

Lucas, her cherished husband, propped his hands on his cane and considered the question for a moment. "We both know that Jamie is not like the average nineteen-year-old."

Victoria couldn't argue that observation. "I've spoken with Jim and Tasha, and they believe it's an excellent step."

Lucas shrugged. "Well, they are her parents. If they're comfortable, we should be as well, I suppose."

Lucas leaned back in his chair, setting his cane to the side. "Perhaps we should begin with a trial period. Three to six months, whichever you believe is best. We can revisit our concerns at that time. If all is well, then we'll continue. If not, we can always put someone else in charge of the program."

Victoria took a breath. "All right. When she arrives, we'll brief her and see how she feels about our suggestions."

Lucas nodded. "Agreed." He stroked his chin a moment. "Did I hear Ian say Eva and Todd Christian were getting married the end of this month?"

"They are," Victoria confirmed. "Bella and Devon are making plans for early next year. They're planning a beautiful wedding in Aspen. Eva and Todd prefer a small wedding and a long honeymoon."

Lucas frowned. "Why am I always the last one to know?"

Victoria laughed. "You are certainly not the last one to know, Lucas. You've just been preoccupied with other things."

He grunted. "I suppose Traynor and Dr. Frasier will be next."

Victoria nodded. "I have no doubt. Love, as you know, comes in its own time."

"That I do." His gray eyes twinkled with mischief. "Ours certainly took quite the journey."

"It did indeed."

A soft rap on the door preceded Jamie's entrance. Victoria's heart leaped as her granddaughter entered the room. Like her father, she had the blond hair and blue eyes of a Colby. She was tall and thin, but strong and incredibly intelligent. Victoria could not be more proud of her.

"Good morning, little girl," Lucas teased. He'd always called Jamie *little girl.*

Jamie leaned down and gave him a peck on the cheek. "Morning, Grandfather." She rounded Victoria's desk and gave her a kiss on the cheek, as well. "You look beautiful as always, Grandmother."

"Thank you, sweetheart. Shall we begin?"

"I can't wait." Jamie settled into the chair next to Lucas. The blue suit she wore set off her beautiful eyes.

"As you're aware," Victoria began, "we've been working with Missing, the international network focused solely on finding missing persons."

"Yes."

It was impossible not to see the excitement in her eyes.

"The Colby Agency is very excited to be a part of the plan to broaden and deepen the search for those who've gone missing, especially the most vulnerable. Since many of the most vulnerable are children and young adults, we have decided it's imperative that someone who can better fit into that world should oversee this new outreach program."

Jamie nodded. "A reasonable conclusion."

"The program will be small in the beginning.

Since the work will be completely pro bono, we need to be quite selective in the cases we choose."

"If our program is successful," Jamie offered, "I'm certain we'll be able to extend the scope of it with funds from generous donors."

There was another of Jamie's uncanny skills. Fund-raising. The girl had a flair for the work. By the time she was in high school, she was already working for half a dozen local charities.

"For now, we'll take it one step at a time," Lucas cautioned. "This is hard, emotionally charged work. Your grandmother and I want to be absolutely certain that you comprehend the challenge before you."

"This is what I want to do," Jamie assured him. "I can think of no more fulfilling work than to reunite the lost with their loved ones."

"There isn't always a happy ending," Victoria cautioned. "Oftentimes, finding those who are lost means finding remains or merely finding the truth and nothing else."

Jamie squared her shoulders and lifted her chin in defiance of their warnings. "I understand and I'm ready to face those challenges."

"It's a fine cause, Jamie," Victoria said, finding it difficult to keep her voice steady. This was a very emotional subject for her. "You've made it clear that you feel deeply about this program. Does what happened to your father have anything to do with those feelings?"

Though Jamie had only heard the stories, she understood what a nightmare that time had been. Her father, Jim, had been stolen from Victoria when he was only seven years old and he remained missing, presumed dead, for more than two decades. Victoria felt certain she would never know all the horrors he had suffered. His journey back to Victoria had not been easy for either of them, but they had survived. Now he had a wonderful wife and two beautiful children, Jamie and her younger brother, Luke. Jim worked alongside Victoria at this agency—the agency she and his father, James Colby, had built. Even now, thinking of those awful years had tears burning her eyes.

"Of course, my decision is rooted in my father's history," Jamie said. "I want to do all within my power to ensure no other child has to go through that nightmare. I know I can't save them all. But I will save everyone that I can. This is how I choose to spend my life, Grandmother. Please help me do that."

"Done." Victoria smiled. "You may begin organizing your team right away."

Jamie hugged them both.

It was a good decision. Victoria's heart was full with the realization that her son and her granddaughter would carry on the work that meant so very much to her.

A new generation of Colbys. Time to celebrate.

* * * * *

Look for more new Colbys coming soon from Debra Webb and Harlequin Intrigue.

To read the story of the return of Victoria's son, look for STRIKING DISTANCE, only from Debra Webb and Harlequin Books.

SPECIAL EXCERPT FROM
HARLEQUIN®

INTRIGUE

Tragedy in her past has made Omega Sector's SWAT team leader Lillian Muir determined to never get attached again—which is easier said than done when ex-flame Jace Eakins walks back into her life. Now, with a mole in their midst, Lillian will have to rely on this newest Omega agent to have her back. Without losing her heart.

Read on for a sneak preview of
ARMED RESPONSE,
the next chapter in the
***OMEGA SECTOR: UNDER SIEGE** series from*
Janie Crouch!

She couldn't see the bastard behind her but knew he was waiting. Waiting to watch her die as her strength gave out and she couldn't support herself anymore.

She tried to yell—even if someone came rushing into the room, it wasn't going to do much more damage than her swaying here until her strength gave out—but the sound was cut off by the rope over her vocal cords. If she wanted to yell, she was going to have to use one hand to pull the rope away from the front of her throat. That meant supporting all her weight with one arm.

Her muscles were already straining from the constant state of pulling up. Supporting her weight with one arm wasn't going to work.

But she'd be damned if she was just going to die in front of this bastard.

HIEXP0718

She swung her legs up, trying to catch the upper part of the rope, but failed again. Even if she could get her legs hooked up there, she wasn't going to be able to get herself released.

She heard a low chuckle to her side. Bastard. He was enjoying this.

And then the alarm started blaring.

Masked Man muttered a curse and took off up the stairs. Lillian felt her arms begin to shake as the exhaustion from holding her own weight began to take its toll. If it wasn't for the rigorous SWAT training, she'd already be dead.

But even training wouldn't be enough. Physics would win. Her arms began to tremble more and she was forced to let go of the rope to give them a break.

Immediately the rope cut off all oxygen.

When everything began to go black, she reached up and grabbed the rope again. It wasn't long before the tremors took over.

She didn't want to go out like this. Wished she hadn't squandered this second chance she'd had with Jace in her life.

But even thinking of Jace, with his gorgeous blue eyes and cocky grin that still did things to her heart after all these years, couldn't give her any more strength.

She reached back up with her arms and found them collapsing before she even took her weight. Then the noose tightened and jerked around her neck, pulling her body forward, all air gone.

Blackness.

Will Jace and the team get there in time to rescue her? Find out when USA TODAY *bestselling author Janie Crouch's ARMED RESPONSE goes on sale August 2018.*
Look for it wherever Harlequin® Intrigue books are sold!

SPECIAL EXCERPT FROM

An engagement of convenience might be the only thing that can save his family's ranch, but Lucian Granger's sudden attraction to his bride-to-be, Karlee O'Malley, will change everything he thought he knew about love...

Enjoy a sneak peek at THE LAST RODEO, *part of the* ***A WRANGLER'S CREEK NOVEL*** *series by* USA TODAY *bestselling author Delores Fossen.*

Karlee walked out onto the ground of the barn where Lucian had busted his butt eighteen times while competing in the rodeo. Perhaps he saw this party as a metaphorical toss from a bronc, but if so, there was no trace of that in his expression. He smiled, his gaze sliding over her, making her thankful she'd opted for a curve-hugging dress and the shoes.

Lucian walked toward her, and the moment he reached her, he curved his arm around her waist, pulled her to him.

And he kissed her.

The world dissolved. That included the ground beneath her feet and every bone in her body. This wasn't like the other stiff kiss in his office. Heck, this wasn't like any other kiss that'd happened—ever.

The feel of him raced through Karlee, and what damage the lip-lock didn't do, his scent finished off. Leather and cowboy. A heady mix when paired with his mouth that she was certain could be classified as one of the deadly sins.

She heard the crowd erupt into pockets of cheers, but all of that noise faded. The only thing was the soft sound

PHEXPDF0718

of pleasure she made. Lucian made a sound, too. A manly grunt. It went well with that manly grip he had on her and his manly taste. Jameson whiskey and sex. Of course, that sex taste might be speculation on her part since the kiss immediately gave her many, many sexual thoughts.

Lucian eased back from her. “You did good,” he whispered.

That dashed the sex thoughts. It dashed a lot of things because it was a reminder that this was all for show. But Lucian didn’t move away from her after saying that. He just stood there, looking down at her with those scorcher blue eyes.

“You did good, too,” Karlee told him because she didn’t know what else to say.

He still didn’t back away despite the fact the applause and cheers had died down and the crowd was clearly waiting for something else to happen. Karlee was waiting, as well. Then it happened.

Lucian kissed her again.

This time, though, it wasn’t that intense smooch. He just brushed his mouth over hers. Barely a touch but somehow making it the most memorable kiss in the history of kisses. Ditto for the long, lingering look he gave her afterward.

“That was from me,” he said, as if that clarified things. It didn’t. It left Karlee feeling even more aroused. And confused.

What the heck did that mean?

Will this pretend engagement lead to happily-ever-after?

Find out in THE LAST RODEO
by USA TODAY *bestselling author Delores Fossen,*
available now.